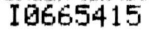

CAMPUS DOLL

A NOVEL BY

EDWIN
WEST

BLACKBIRD BOOKS
NEW YORK • LOS ANGELES

A Blackbird Classic, December 2020

Copyright © 1961 by Edwin West

Manufactured in the United States of America.

The events and characters depicted in this book are fictional.

Cover painting by Tom Miller

Cataloging-in-Publication Data

West, Edwin.
Campus doll / Edwin West.
p. cm.
1. Crime—Fiction. 2. College students—Fiction.
3. Prostitution—Fiction. 5. I. Title.
PS3573.E9 C36 2020 813'.54—dc23 2020952088

Blackbird Books
www.bbirdbooks.com
email us at editor@bbirdbooks.com

ISBN 978-1-61053-046-0

First Blackbird Edition

10 9 8 7 6 5 4 3 2 1

CAMPUS DOLL

1

JACKIE HAYES, tall, slender and well-built, sat half-asleep in Modes of Writing 201, gazing inattentively out the classroom window at the November landscape and absentmindedly doodling on the open page of her notebook. Professor Blake's voice droned on hopelessly, and among the twenty-four students lined around the table there was nary a stir.

Jackie's blue eyes, glazed by animal boredom, traveled their gaze slowly from the window, across the professor's mumbling mouth and the bowed heads of her fellow sufferers, and came to rest, finally, on the result of her doodling. The glaze disappeared from her eyes, she started involuntarily, and her two hands moved together to cover what she'd been drawing.

She hadn't even known she'd been thinking about sex.

She hadn't moved fast enough. Rick Marshall, in the seat at her right, leaned surreptitiously toward her and whispered,

"If that was supposed to be me, you should have made it larger."

Professor Blake said, "What?" It was the most clearly enunciated word he'd said all hour. A tall, gaunt, overly serious man in his early thirties, Blake was inevitably intimidated by his subject matter and his students, and his discomfort was as apparent as his thin nose and spaniel eyes. Look mean at Blake, said the scuttlebutt, and he won't flunk you no matter what.

Jackie saw everyone looking at her, and felt her face turning beet red. Rick, taller and heavier than Blake, his nose flattened from an accident during football practice last year—he was a junior, the same age as Jackie (twenty), and first-string right guard—grinned with easy insolence and drawled, "I just asked her to spell onomatopoeia."

"Is that right?" said Blake sarcastically. This moment had to be, unfortunately, one of Blake's rare attempts at self-assertion. He glared at Jackie's, hands, in their awkward position on the open notebook, obviously covering something, and said, "Writing notes back and forth? Isn't that more of a grade-school stunt than something one would do in college?"

"It isn't a note," said Jackie. She had trouble getting any volume in her voice, and as soon as she stopped speaking she realized just how unfortunate the phrasing was.

"Not a note?" echoed Blake. "Then just what is it?"

Jackie felt like crawling under the table. Everybody was waiting for her to say something. "Just a—just a doodle," she said. "I was just doodling."

"Bring it here," said Blake.

"It's just a doodle," said Jackie desperately. She thought she could kill Rick for getting her into this jam. "Bring it here," repeated Blake.

Unwillingly, Jackie rose and carried the notebook around to the head of the table, where Blake was standing. She handed it to him without a word and waited for the sky to fall.

Blake's face got very red, and he snapped the notebook shut. His eyes searched quickly for the clock on the opposite wall, which said ten minutes before three. "Class dismissed," he said, with obvious relief, handed Jackie's notebook back to her and fled.

Jackie fled, too, before anyone could ask her what the doodle was. Behind her, she could hear Rick call, "Don't forget our date!"

"Seven o'clock," she shouted back, and raced from the building toward the bus stop. Modes of Writing 201— essentially a survey course of British literature up to, but not including, the nineteenth century—was her last class on Friday afternoon, and now she was through with school for the weekend. *And maybe forever,* she thought grimly, remembering the letter and the newspaper clipping from home.

Her bus came—the MG was in the garage today, getting a new muffler—and she stepped aboard, a good-looking blond girl with level eyes, firm shoulders and breasts, an aura of money, determination and purpose, and a tail that twitched provocatively when she walked. Heads usually turned when she passed by.

Home for Jackie Hayes was a four-room furnished apartment seven blocks from the campus here in Clifton, Ohio. Having a banker father in a mill town in New Hampshire, Jackie was used to having money. She neither wanted nor needed the barren confinement of a dormitory room on campus. With the collusion of indulgent parents and an eager no-questions-asked landlady, Mrs. Elsie Bible became Jackie's rather improbable aunt—and it was legal for a coed to live off campus if she lived with a relative.

And now the apartment—fixed up with loving, lavish and expensive care—and the MG—red as sin and twice as fast—and even the college itself were all very probably going to be taken away from Jackie Hayes. And all because her father was an idiot.

Coming into the apartment now—it occupied the complete second floor over a dry cleaning establishment—Jackie's eye fell immediately on the letter and the newspaper clipping on the coffee table in the living room. She'd had the letter only two days, but it had already been read so many times, so often folded and refolded and twisted in nervous fingers, that it was now dog-eared and tearing at the creases.

The letter was from Jackie's mother, in her normal, infuriatingly vague style, full of half-hints and premonitions, managing in its own meandering way to get across the idea that something was up on the home front, and that that something had a lot to do with money, and that when the something—whatever it was—had run its course the Hayes family might very well be broke. The circumstances were only hinted at, and the hints could have referred to everything or anything, from the Industrial Revolution to World War III.

The newspaper clipping had come in a scuffed and dirty envelope with Jackie's home-town postmark on it, and with the clipping there had been a small piece of lined note paper with, "You ought to be interested in this. A Well Wisher" scrawled on it in pencil.

The clipping, from her home-town newspaper, elaborated on the hints in her mother's letter. The mill which had historically been the town's one and only excuse for existence had moved just recently to South Carolina, taking with it only the most useful skilled labor and leaving behind it a town where the people remaining had nothing left to do but take in each other's wash. Money was tight, the local bank was crammed with people withdrawing their savings and, in the resulting confusion, some financial shenanigans had been discovered. Someone—the clipping didn't care to name names—had been embezzling funds on a grand and consistent scale over a period of fifteen or twenty years.

So that was that. Jackie's father had apparently never been content with his salary, substantial as it was, and now the balloon had burst. And if Jackie knew the local burghers, her father wouldn't be going to jail. That wasn't their way. They'd simply strip him of every penny he had and wash their hands of the affair.

Which meant it was good-bye college, good-bye lovely apartment and good-bye MG.

The letter and the clipping had come in the same mail, two days ago. Since then, she had spent her time at home worrying about it and cursing her father—not for his stupidity but for his clumsiness in getting caught—and her time away from the apartment in a relatively successful attempt to ignore and forget the whole thing.

Today's mail should have brought her weekly allowance check. The mailbox, when she'd checked it just now, had been empty. The boom had fallen. She would probably get the letter on Monday, telling her that she was going to have to give up college and come home.

Home. Brickville, New Hampshire wasn't home. It had never been home, not really; she'd hated the town all her life. And for the last two and a half years Clifton, Ohio and Clifton College had been her home. Brickville had simply been the place where the money came from.

Go back to Brickville? She hated the thought.

Hating it, she forced it to the back of her mind. The end wouldn't come before Monday, so she had at least one more weekend here before she would have to face the result of her father's stupidity.

And tonight there was Rick Marshall.

Rick was a lot of fun. For some reason or other, they'd never gotten together at all during their first two years at college, and it wasn't until last month, when the fall semester of their junior year started, that they ever went out together.

And tonight, in a way, was going to be the culmination of their dating. They both knew it, and now that she thought about it she realized that that was undoubtedly the subconscious thought behind that stupid doodle she'd drawn in Blake's class.

Thinking about Rick excited her, and helped her ignore the threat of the letter and the clipping. She was going to enjoy Rick, she knew it already, for she hadn't gone to bed with anyone since May, six months before.

Though she hadn't been a virgin for three years or more, Jackie had never been in any way promiscuous. She considered sex an inevitable—and very enjoyable—part of going steady, but certainly not something to be shared with just anybody who happened along. This wasn't a moral judgment, but simply the ethic of her group and she went happily along with it.

As she would do tonight. May was a long time ago, and Rick was a lot of fun to be with, and Monday was millions of years away. By the time Jackie had stripped and was in the shower, her spirits had revived to the point where she could raise her voice above the roar of the shower and sing out with the rawest drinking song she knew.

When Rick came for her at seven, she looked her best and she knew it. Her blond hair was carefully upswept, her firm and slender figure was outlined sharply beneath a full-skirted black cocktail dress, and her legs—they were good legs, strong legs, legs she was proud of—were sheathed in nylon and mounted on black spike-heel shoes. Her only make-up was lipstick, and it was all she needed.

She still had most of her summer tan, which contrasted beautifully with her blond hair and black dress. And a narrow intricately carved bracelet in white gold on her left wrist was her only jewelry for the occasion.

Rick pounded up the stairs to the second floor precisely at seven, hallooing joyously all the way up. There was never any worry about noise in this apartment, which was the main reason Jackie had chosen it. The building was only two stories high, and the dry cleaning place on the first floor closed every afternoon at six. It was a corner building, so there were no neighbors to the left, and on the right it was flanked by a grammar school.

Rick burst through the door at the head of the stairs, grinning, and cried, "Hiya, Jackie! Done any more doodling?"

Having finally come to a stop in the middle of the living room, he struck a self-conscious pose, shoulders straight, chest semi-expanded, arms slightly cocked at the elbows. He was tall, heavy, broad-shouldered and chunkily muscular all over his body except for his legs, which were thin and white and straggled with limp black hair.

He was proud of his chest and shoulders, embarrassed by his legs, and altogether too much aware of his body. He almost never made an unconscious movement, and he took such good care of his body that he was virtually on a training program all year long, with one exception, and Jackie was a good example of the exception.

"If you hadn't opened your big mouth," Jackie told him, in answer to his crack about the doodling, "Blake would never have caught on."

Rick laughed, clapping his hands together in a careful arm movement, so that his shoulders didn't for a second leave their straight alignment. When he laughed, he opened his mouth wide and cocked his head to one side, which caused a ridge of muscle to spring into prominence along the side of his thick neck. It was a movement he had practiced before a mirror, and he rather liked the effect.

"Did you see old Blake's face," he cried joyously, "when he saw that goddamn doodle? I thought he was going to fall down in a faint!"

This time Jackie laughed with him. "I thought I was going to fall down in a faint," she said. "I could see myself trying to explain to Dean Kelland what that doodle of mine had to do with the historic plays of Christopher Marlowe."

His voice softened, his smile got closer to a leer, and he took a step toward her. "Just what made you decide to draw that doodle in the first place, honey-girl?"

She shook her head, taking his question seriously. "I don't know," she replied. "I don't know what got into me."

He said, "Ha!" and she said, "You know what I meant. Don't be silly."

He took another step forward, so that now he could reach out both hands and gently touch her forearms. "What were you thinking about instead of old Chris Marlowe, honey-girl? Were you thinking about little old me?"

"Look at the time," she said, moving deftly away from him. "We have to go pick up the car and everything before the movie. What's playing tonight?"

"What do you say we forget about the movie tonight," he suggested, following her around the room.

"Take it easy, bullyboy," she said, only half kidding with him. "Don't go rushing things all of a sudden. One of the qualities I've liked most about you is your sense of timing."

He stopped then, nodded his head slowly, as though it were too massive to go any faster, and grinned with one side of his mouth. "Right you are," he said. "That damn doodle of yours threw me off my stride."

"You? What about Blake?"

"Ha!"

"What's at the movie?" she asked again, shrugging into her coat.

He shook his head. "Some dog called *A Sound of Distant Drums*. It's either a Korean War thing or a Western, I forget."

"We'll go anyway," she said. "And we'd better hurry if we want to pick up the car."

As they went out the door to the stairs, he slapped her on the rump and said, "How come we never got together until this year, honey-girl?"

"I don't know," she said. "Kismet, I guess."

"Yeah, and I guess we've got some lost time to make up for."

His saying that reminded Jackie suddenly of the letter and the clipping. Lost time. It was going to be all lost time from now on, nothing but lost time. Monday and every day after that. "Then we'd better hurry and catch up," she said, and trotted quickly down the stairs to the street.

It turned out to be a double feature—a Korean War picture *and* a Western, both bad, and it was almost midnight before they got out of the theater. Rick wanted to go on back to Jackie's place right away, but Jackie felt time pressing more and more closely around her.

To go back to her place would be to admit that Friday was over, that there were only two days left now instead of three, and then it would be Monday. She didn't want Friday to be over. "Let's go for a ride first," she suggested. "Let's drive out to Ogilvie's and get a drink before we go home."

"Ogilvie's? That joint will be crowded tonight, a real mess. You don't want to go there, honey-girl." He put an arm around her shoulders and they strolled toward the car. "Let's just go on to your place," he said.

"I want to go get a drink at Ogilvie's," she insisted. She was getting annoyed at Rick for trying to end Friday so soon, and so she spoke more sharply than she intended.

"What's the matter?" he asked her. "Don't you have anything to drink at your place?"

"I don't feel like going home yet, Rick," she said. She stopped beside the car and glared at him. "If you're in a hurry to go home," she added, "you go right ahead. I want to go to Ogilvie's."

He shrugged—carefully—and grinned. "No need to chop my head off, honey-girl," he said. "Ogilvie's it is."

Jackie got behind the wheel, Rick settled into the bucket seat beside her, and the MG spun away from the curb and down across the intersection, headed for the highway.

Clifton, Ohio was on Route 68, just about midway between Springfield and Xenia. Ogilvie's, a rambling bar with log cabin decor inside and out, was a college crowd hangout about a mile and a half from town toward Springfield.

When they arrived, the parking lot at the side was crammed with cars, and the interior was filled with the Clifton College student body. Pushing their way through the crowd, nodding and shouting hello to the people they recognized, they finally found two empty chairs—no table, though—near the back. They sat down, facing one another, the wall right beside them, and Rick leaned forward to yell over the din, "I'll try and get up to the bar. I'll be back as quick as I can."

She shook her head and at his look of puzzlement she leaned forward and shouted, "I don't want anything to drink now. Let's just sit here."

"What the hell for?" he demanded, but she made believe she didn't hear him.

They stayed at Ogilvie's for about ten minutes, but then it got too painful for Jackie to stand. At first, she had enjoyed the familiar crowd and the familiar bedlam in the familiar hangout—being here, she was still a part of it—but gradually it came home to her that next weekend she wouldn't be here, that this place would be part of her past by then and that all the people she had smiled and waved and called at on her way through the place tonight would already be saying to one another, "Remember Jackie Hayes?"

Jackie Hayes was not the kind of girl who cried readily, but she could feel the tears of frustration, rage and premature nostalgia building up behind her eyes. At last, she grabbed Rick's hand and pushed quickly through the crowd again to the front door, looking neither right nor left and not acknowledging any of the greetings shouted at her.

Once in the car, she drove violently, mashing the accelerator to the floor boards, screaming around the curves of this winding trunk road, heading not back toward Clifton but on toward Springfield. Rick tried to talk to her once or twice, but she paid no attention to him. Finally he gave up and devoted full time to clinging to the bucket seat.

On the last curve before the town line of Springfield, Jackie cut in too fast and made the turn a fraction of a second too late. The right rear wheel scraped across the roadway and ground into the gravel shoulder, spinning madly, rocking the car. Jackie fought the wheel, gradually got the car back under control and slowed down. "God-damn!" breathed Rick, shaken into a completely uncharacteristic limp sprawl in the bucket seat. Jackie ignored him and made a U-turn at the next opportunity.

Going back to Clifton, she still drove rapidly but much more sensibly. Her foot did occasionally touch the brake. They passed Ogilvie's again and Jackie grimaced, then muttered, "I'm sorry. I got upset and kind of mad—when I'm like that I like to drive hard."

"Was it anything I did, Jackie?" Rick was still shaken, too much so to remember to call her honey-girl.

She shook her head. "It wasn't you. Never mind. It was just a mood. I'm all right now."

"I think maybe I could use a little drink after all," said Rick slowly.

She glanced at him and smiled, then looked back at the highway. "I've got some gin at home," she said. "But you'll have to mix it with water. I don't have any kind of mixer."

"I'll mix it with an ice cube," he told her. "That's plenty good enough for me."

They drove to Jackie's place, leaving the MG in its usual spot at the curb. Theoretically, there was a parking ban in Clifton from two to five a.m., but the Clifton police force was an industrious crew, particularly the night shift, and most of them had a number of private concerns to take their attention, so Jackie's MG had never been tagged for violating the ban.

They went up the dark stairs to the second floor, and it is a mark of Rick's intimidation by Jackie's strange actions that, though she went up the stairs first, he didn't lay a hand on her.

Upstairs, she fixed two drinks, gin on the rocks for both of them, and they sat together on the sofa. At his wary expression, she laughed and said, "I'm all right now. It was just some bad news from home, nothing to worry about. Don't look so frightened."

"I'm not frightened," he said quickly. "I just didn't know what you were going to do next."

"Then I'll tell you," she said. "I'm going to sit here beside you and drink my gin, like a good girl. What are *you* going to do next?"

"This." He put the glass down on an end table and reached for her.

She came into his arms readily, closing her eyes as his arms encircled her, hands brushing her back, lips pressing with gentle insistence on hers. She parted her lips for him and lightly curled her fingers at the back of his neck, knowing that that particular woman's touch always made a man more excited.

"You could draw from life," he whispered, but she said, "Ssshhh, don't talk," and kissed him again. She wanted to hide his imperfections from herself, not see them, cover them one way or another. This was to be the last weekend, almost the last night, and it had to be good.

When she felt his hand at the side zipper of her dress, she stiffened for just a second, then forced herself to relax. For all his careful fluid movement, there was something awkward and fumbling about Rick, and this was the worst time in the world to think about it.

She succeeded in driving all thought out of her mind— of Rick, of her parents, the college and even of herself. She was no more and no less than a body, now a willing, demanding female body, in the arms of a man, being touched and caressed and kissed and made love to.

Her body quivered at his touch. The male fingers undressed the female form, and the male arms, slow and strong, lifted her and carried her through the darkness to the bedroom. The man sought and found her, and her body exploded in unthinking sensation.

Later she cried the tears she had been holding back, refusing to acknowledge the existence of, for the last two days all came boiling up in a rush and she wept wrackingly, her body quivering on the bed. His hands were rough and awkward as he tried to console her, not knowing why she was crying.

"What is it, Jackie?" he whispered in the darkness. "Jackie, what is it?" But she was crying too hard to answer him.

After fifteen minutes of this, she stopped all at once, as though a button had been pushed, a lever turned, and she rolled over onto her back beside him, staring up through the pitch-black darkness toward where the ceiling would be if the light were on, and tonelessly she said, "Give me a cigarette, Ricky." She had never called him Ricky before. No one had, for twelve years or more.

But all he said was, "All right." He got out of bed and stumbled across to the door separating the two rooms. In the living room, he hunted futilely for his clothes for a minute, found a table lamp, and switched it on.

From the bedroom she cried at once, "Turn it off!"

He obeyed, but in the few seconds the light had been on he'd discovered his clothing. He searched the pockets, found his cigarettes and matches, and lit two cigarettes before returning to the bedroom, knowing instinctively that even the light from a match would be too much for Jackie right now.

Back in the bedroom he saw that the darkness wasn't quite complete. The bed sheets stood out as a lighter black in the blackness and Jackie, now sitting up with her back against the headboard, was barely visible framed by that lighter blackness. "Here," he said and handed her one of the cigarettes.

"Thank you."

He settled into the bed again, sitting beside her, their shoulders and hips barely touching. They smoked in silence for a while, until Jackie finally sighed and shook her head and said, "I'm sorry, Rick."

"That's okay," he said, but there was still wariness in his voice.

"No, it isn't okay. I wanted this to be good—I wanted it to be extra special. And it could have been—you're awful good, Rick, do you know that?—but I just got this mood on me and I guess I ruined everything."

"Do you want to talk about it, honey-girl?" he asked. He was beginning to get his confidence back. She wasn't an anonymous, hurricane-like force, after all, he reasoned. She was just a girl with a bad mood on.

"What good would it do to talk?"

"I'm a great listener," he prompted.

She sighed, shook her head again, inhaled on the cigarette. Finally, she said, "I'm going to have to leave school."

"Leave school?"

"And sell the car, too, you can bet anything. And go home to Brickville. *Brickville!*" She said it the second time as though it were a curse.

"Why? And when? What the hell is all this, Jackie?"

"When? I'll probably get the word Monday."

"You mean you're being kicked out?"

She laughed bitterly. "I wish it was as easy as that, Rick."

"Then what the hell is it, honey-girl? Tell old Rick."

"My father," she said, her voice quick and flat and emotionless, "is an embezzler. And an idiot. A bank president embezzler."

"What the hell—?"

She reached out suddenly and flicked on the lamp on the night stand, catching Rick with an expression of befuddled amazement on his face. She laughed at him and said, "We were probably driving around on stolen funds tonight, Ricky. What do you think of that?"

"I don't get it," he said frankly.

"Come on," she said. She sprang up from the bed, lithe and tanned, except for the two pale strips over her breasts, belly and buttocks, where she had worn her bathing suit. Her pink-tipped breasts moved as she walked, without flabbiness, the muscles writhing beneath the taut skin of her hips. She strode around the bed and on into the living room. Rick followed her, frowning, no longer sure it was such a good idea to be a great listener, but knowing he was stuck with it now.

She sat on the sofa, brushed her bra off the sofa onto the floor and said, "Sit down. Take a look at these."

He sat beside her and accepted the letter and clipping she handed him. He read through her mother's letter with obvious puzzlement, looked at her with bewilderment plain in his eyes and read the letter all the way through again. Then he read the clipping twice. Finished, he returned them both to the coffee table and sat back. "And you figure," he said, "they'll make your Old Man pay it all back?"

"I know they will."

He frowned. "Couldn't you get a job?"

"To support this place? And the car? *And* still go to school?"

He nodded slowly, agreeing with her, then said, "There's one way you—No, forget it, it was a nutty idea."

"What was it?" she demanded.

"You wouldn't want to do it," he said. "Forget it. It was just a nutty idea, that's all."

"I'd want to do it," she said positively. "I'd want to do anything that could let me go on living here the way I'm used to, that could fix it so I wouldn't have to go back to that lousy Brickville, now or ever, that could let me keep this place and the MG and still go to college at the same time. I'd do anything if I could have all that, but there just isn't any way and that's all there is to it."

He gave her a sidelong glance. "How serious are you, Jackie?"

"How serious do you think I am?"

"Yeah," he said. "Well, listen, this was just something that occurred to me, that's all. I mean, don't get mad at me for saying it. It was just a nutty idea that—"

"Oh, cut out the preamble," she snapped. "Either tell me or get off the pot."

"Yeah," he said again. He sneaked a look at her once more, then studied the opposite wall. "Stop giving it away for free," he said.

"What?"

He jerked his head at the bedroom door. "That. Stop giving it away for free."

There was a long silence. He glanced at her again from the corner of his eye, to see her staring at him blank-faced. The silence emboldened him and he said, "There's plenty of guys on campus would like to get a piece of you, honey-girl. You could make a good living, you know? And it wouldn't take much of your time, either." He looked at her fully. "What do you think of the idea?"

Slowly, her expression changed. She smiled, nodded, then held her hand out to him. "That'll be ten dollars, Ricky," she said.

2

JACKIE SAT at her usual table in the Student Union, a cold cup of tea at her elbow. It was a Thursday in late November, three weeks after her conversation with Rick Marshall. Her regular appointment time on Thursdays was between one and two in the afternoon, and here it was ten minutes to two and not a single customer had shown up yet. Most of the regulars she'd collected in the last three weeks had already signed up for next week, but there were still three time slots open, two on Wednesday and one on Thursday.

Jackie was working five nights a week, scheduling three customers a night for an hour each, between the hours of nine and midnight, at ten dollars apiece, for a total of one hundred fifty dollars a week.

The original idea had been Rick's, true enough, but the details had been Jackie's all the way down the line. "You spread the word in the boys' dorms," she'd told him, "but for God's sake be careful who you talk to.

If a word of this gets out, we'll all be booted out of college and maybe thrown into jail besides."

"Don't worry about me," he'd said easily. "I know who to talk to and who not."

"I hope so," she'd murmured dubiously. There was no likelihood of Jackie ever overrating Rick. "We'll make appointments in advance," she said. "I don't intend to go prowling around on the streets, and I'm not going to have a whole mob show up here at once for any gang bang or anything like that."

Rick had grinned admiringly at her. "Appointments in advance," he had echoed. "My God, Jackie, you've got a hell of a mind. How come you never thought of this yourself?"

"I don't know," she had said, seriously considering the question. "It's a natural, once you stop to think about it."

"It sure as hell is."

Eight minutes to two and still no customers.

She had outlined the operation to Rick all that night. It had started to develop in her mind almost the very instant he had suggested the idea. "They'll get an hour," she had said, "for ten dollars. Three guys a night—just Monday through Friday. That should give me enough to live on."

He had frowned at that. "Only ten bucks? You could get a hell of a lot more than that, Jackie."

She had shaken her head. "The guys in school don't have a lot of money," she had told him. "Ten dollars is just about as much as they'll want to spend."

"What about local customers?" he had asked her. "People from Clifton, maybe even from Springfield and Xenia."

"No," she had said. "College students only, and only by appointment. And if I don't know the guy, he's going to have to show me his Activity Card to prove he's a student at Clifton."

Rick had burst into laughter. "Activity Card! Holy jumping flatheads, Activity Card! And what an activity, huh, Jackie?"

"I don't want to get any of the occupational diseases of this trade," she had explained seriously. "And I'll be safest if I stick to students. Oh, and that reminds me. There are little things you can buy—they're for the prevention of disease. The customer has to furnish his own, or it's no sale. There's one disease I don't want to get and that's a baby."

Six minutes to two and still no customers.

"What about making these appointments?" Rick had asked her.

"Just a second."

She had found the copy of her course schedule, and checked to see when her free daytime hours were. "I'll be in the Student Union," she had told him, "at one of the tables in the back, drinking tea, for an hour every day. Let's see, Monday, Wednesday and Friday from three to four, and Tuesday and Thursday from one to two. That's when they can make the appointments."

"Goddamn, what a business woman!" he had cried in honest admiration.

Four minutes to two and still no customers. But Jackie noticed again the nervous little kid who'd been hanging around by the entrance for the last ten or fifteen minutes. A customer, she told herself, and he's trying to build up his nerve.

As Rick was leaving that night three weeks ago, she had said, "You spread the word over the weekend, and I'll start making the appointments Monday afternoon. But be sure you're careful who you tell."

"I'll be careful, honey-girl, don't you worry." He had grinned and patted her rump again.

"By the way," she had said, "there's a little matter of ten dollars."

His smile had faded and she had laughed into the silence. "You're my first customer, Rick. Isn't that something to pay for?"

"Okay," he said reluctantly and, more reluctantly still, had dragged out his wallet and counted into her hand a five and five singles. Putting the wallet away, he had said, "That's because this time was special, like you say. But next time, it's free."

"You told me not to give it away for free any more, Rick."

"Honey-girl, it was my idea. The least you can do—the *very* least—is give me a special deal. Like for free."

From the expression on his face, she had known it would be dangerous to argue with him. "All right, Rick," she had said. "You're right. Next time is for free."

"There you go, honey-girl. Now you're talking sense again."

She had known she was talking sense. Rick was her only approach to her customers. So she had—much as it went against the grain—extended the ten dollars out to him. "Here. This one was for free, too. For having the idea."

He had shaken his head. "No, no, honey-girl, you hold on to that money. It's the first and last time you'll ever get any dough from me. *That's* something special, too, isn't it?" And he had laughed and pounded down the stairs and away.

Two minutes to two, and the nervous little kid approached the table. Jackie smiled at him, encouraging him to come on. The kid looked like a freshman, no more than seventeen, short and skinny and pale, pimpled and bespectacled. He had the face, arms and torso that belonged with Rick Marshall's legs. He also had the legs.

He finally reached the table and, in a voice that had changed once but had now apparently decided to change back again, he squeaked, "Are you Jackie?"

"Sure, I am," she said, smiling at him even more. In the last three weeks, she had become a professional in more ways than one. She was now, among other things, a professional at putting scared little mice like this one here at their ease. "Sit down here with me," she said, keeping her voice soft, so it reached him but none of the other coffee and doughnut eating students at the surrounding tables.

He sat down in a jerky, collapsing movement, as though someone invisible had suddenly kicked him into the chair, and immediately started talking with desperate speed, while his voice changed back and forth at a maddening pace, as though he were trying to be a whole barber-shop quartet all by himself. "Maybe it was a gag," he blurted. "I'm not sure, but they said it was on the level, and if it's a gag don't get sore or anything like that. I wasn't even going to come here, but everybody told me it was really on the level. If it's a gag you just tell me and not get mad or anything and I'll just go right away and leave you alone because—"

He ran out of breath, finally, and into his gulping silence Jackie said, "It isn't a gag, uh . . . what did you say your name was?"

"Bert," he said. It was more of a bark than a name.

"Bert," she echoed. "Hi. I'm Jackie." And she took his cold, limp, sweating and unresisting hand and shook it in firm comradeship.

"And it isn't a gag?" he demanded. It was hard to tell whether he was happy or sad about that. Jackie supposed he was probably both. He'd wanted to, but he'd been afraid to. If it had turned out to be a gag he'd have been able to tell himself that he had dared, and it wasn't his fault that he wasn't allowed to go through with it.

"It isn't a gag, Bert," she said. "Do you suppose I could see your Activity Card? I mean, you understand, I'm not accusing you of anything, but we've never met before, and I want to be sure you're really a student."

"Oh," he said, and got so flustered he reached both hands back to his two back pants-pockets simultaneously. After a bone-snapping struggle his right hand emerged triumphant with a wallet. Opening the wallet was another problem, but finally he had it open to the proper leaf and he proudly set the wallet down on the table in front of Jackie, with the Activity Card showing, upside down.

Jackie, keeping her smile constant, turned the wallet around. "I'm a freshman," said Bert, as though that explained everything, and it did.

The Activity Card was written out to a Bert Abnerhauf, and this quivering reed across the table from her was a Bert Abnerhauf if she'd ever seen one. "Okay," she said. "It's ten dollars, you know. You have to pay me now."

She reached for her notebook to check her schedule. The first time slot she mentioned—ten p.m. on Wednesday—he agreed to at once, and slipped her the ten dollars—

surprisingly, a crisp new ten-dollar bill, obviously fresh from the bank—and raced away as though his pants were on fire.

She looked after him, grinning, and wondered if he'd show up. She had a feeling he wouldn't. That had happened a few times already, and was an unexpected advantage to this appointment-in-advance system. There were some frightened little boys who could nerve themselves to the supreme effort once, but not twice. They paid their money and they took their appointments, but they never showed up to claim the merchandise and they never showed up to ask for their money back. Boys like that gave Jackie extra odd hours of rest during the week, and it looked very much as though ten to eleven o'clock this Wednesday would be a good time to do some homework.

Jackie was late for her two o'clock class. It was a General Science lab and nobody cared, so it was all right. Nobody cared that she left half an hour early, either, at four-thirty, since half the other students in the class left around that time as well. Their teacher, Professor Meyer, was writing a book on molecular saturation, or some such thing, and students were just an interruption to his day's writing.

She drove the MG home and found a letter from her mother in the mailbox. The letter she had expected on that fateful Monday three weeks ago had shown up on schedule, and she had replied to it with a glowing letter, all about the part-time private secretary job she had found, which would make it possible for her to stay in school. Her mother was delighted by this. Her father had made no comment. He hadn't written any letters at all since the fiasco, probably out of shame, and Jackie thought he certainly should have every right to be ashamed. His own bank and he couldn't figure out a way to steal from it without getting caught.

She had received no more clippings from the Well Wisher, either. Her mother was as vague as ever, so she had no new information on the state of crime in Brickville, and she couldn't possibly have cared less.

Holding the as-yet-unopened new letter from her mother in the same hand as her schoolbooks, she opened the ground-floor door next to the dry-cleaning window, and started up the stairs, then stopped dead.

Ed Warner was sitting on the top step, waiting for her, his back against the door.

The first Tuesday, the second day she'd been accepting appointments, she'd been warned about Ed Warner. Marty Jukovsky, a senior, had given her the word. "Ed took a little trip into Mexico this summer," he had told her, "and he picked up a girl. From her he picked up a little present. He says he's cured, but we don't want to take any chances, you know what I mean?"

"I know just what you mean," Jackie had told him. "I don't want to take any chances, either."

And she hadn't. Ed Warner had showed up two days later, asking for an appointment, and she had told him no. When he asked her why, she told him the truth, but hadn't mentioned Marty's name. Ed had insisted that he was cured, but she had said, "I can't afford to take the chance. If the word gets around that I said yes to you, I'll lose all my other customers. They'll all be afraid to come to me. I'm sorry, Ed, but there's no way around it. I just can't take the chance."

"Damnit," he had cried, "I told you it's all right now! What the hell is this?"

"I can't," she had insisted.

"You goddamn well better," he had said, his voice low and threatening. He had leaned forward across the table and said, "If you don't want Dean Kelland to find out what the hell you're up to, then you had goddamn well better take the chance."

"I have a lot of customers," she had told him calmly, looking him in the eye. "If Dean Kelland finds out about me, they'll know that you're the only one who could have told him. And I think they'll make you sorry you did any talking."

He had blustered and raged, but she had stayed calm and adamant. Finally he had given up and gone stomping away, a stocky, redheaded, angry-faced boy with hairy hands and a simian walk.

And now he was sitting just outside her door—the expression on his face was one of grim determination.

Jackie paused on the third step from the bottom, looking up. "What do you want, Ed?"

"You know damn good and well what I want."

"I told you already, Ed. No."

"I don't give a damn what you told me. My money's as good as anybody's" He pulled a crumpled ten-dollar bill from his pocket and flung it down the stairs at her. "There's the ten. Now come up here."

"No, Ed."

"You come up here, or I'll go down and get you." And he took two steps down toward her.

It was the first time in her life that Jackie had ever been seriously threatened. She felt her heart pounding furiously within her chest, and she knew that she was terrified. If she tried to turn around, get down the stairs again and out onto the sidewalk, he would come leaping down the stairs three or four at a time. He'd get to her before she ever reached the door.

And screaming wouldn't do any good. She'd picked this place primarily because she could make all the noise she wanted here and nobody would bother or pay any attention.

She was terrified. She wouldn't be able to fight him off, and afterward he would be sure to tell everybody that he had managed to force her to give in to him, after all, and her whole business would be shot to hell.

And he might not be really cured.

"Come on," he growled. "Come on the hell up here. I'm not going to wait a hell of a lot longer."

"Ed, please," she started.

"The hell with that," he shouted. "I'm the laughingstock of the whole goddamn school. Here's a goddamn broad who's *selling* it, for crissake, and I can't even get any from her. Well, the hell with that!"

"Ed, you'll ruin everything for me. Please, Ed."

"Come the hell up here, goddamn you."

"Ed, listen," she said desperately. "Maybe we can work something out."

"You're goddamn right we can work something out," he told her, "And I know just where we can do it, too. On your bed. There's your lousy ten bucks. Pick it up and get up here or I'm coming down after you."

"Ed, wait a minute. You bring me something from a doctor—a paper from a doctor that says you're cured—and it'll be okay. You won't have to force me or anything, and as often as you want. Ed—"

"The hell with that," he shouted, his rage growing. "I want it now, goddamn it!"

She stared up at him, and she knew the truth. "You aren't really cured," she said.

"What the hell do you care whether I'm cured or not, you goddamn whore? You put out for the whole school, baby, and that means you put out for me, too. That's all there is to it."

"Ed, I *can't!*"

"The hell with this talking!" he shouted, and suddenly bounded down the steps. Before she could move, he had a tight, painful grip on her arm, just above the elbow.

"Ed, please . . ."

"Never mind the crap," he said, and started up the stairs, dragging her along after him.

She struggled, but he was strong and enraged, and there was no way for her to escape the grip on her arm. At the top of the stairs, he stopped and said, "Unlock the door."

"No."

The grip on her arm tightened, while his other hand reached across to clutch at a breast. He squeezed with both hands until she cried out, and then he said again, "Unlock the door."

She was shaking so badly she had to try twice before she could get the key into the lock, then he pushed the door open and shoved her through ahead of him.

And Rick, smiling and calm, stood up slowly from the living room sofa, saying, "Okay, Ed-boy, you've had your fun. Now turn around and go right back out again."

"Rick!" cried Jackie, and the name was a prayer of thanksgiving. When Ed's hand released her, she found suddenly that her legs were too weak to support her. She sank to the floor and sat there, gasping for breath, watching the two boys studying one another.

"You get the hell out of here, Marshall," said Ed. "This doesn't have anything to do with you."

"Oh, but it does," said Rick easily. "I'm little Jackie's protector." He smiled down at her and said, "Isn't that right, Jackie?"

She nodded, unable to speak, watching him wide-eyed.

"So that's the way it is, Ed, old boy," said Rick. Still smiling, he strolled across the room toward Ed, his body in a jaunty pose like a combination between complete relaxation and a fighter's stance. "So you just go on home and scratch your sores, boy. You know what I mean?"

"You son of a bitch!" cried Ed, and leaped at Rick, fists flailing.

Rick's smile tightened and his fighter's crouch became more pronounced. He let Ed get in close, and then his fists moved in short, fast deliberate arcs as he circled slowly to the left, around the other boy.

Ed's fighting style was completely unscientific. He simply kept wading in, as dogged as a tank, his fists thudding against Rick's arms and shoulders, while Rick circled carefully to the left, his fists snapping out whenever he saw an opening, his arms moving constantly to keep Ed's fists from getting in too close.

When Rick broke his pattern, he did it so suddenly that Jackie could barely watch the movement. He feinted to the left, then stepped suddenly to the right, pivoted, and his right arm curved up inside Ed's defenses and cracked against the point of Ed's jaw with a sound like a hammer hitting wood.

Ed snapped backward as though he'd been yanked, stumbled against a chair, and fell heavily to the floor. But he rolled away immediately, came up again, his face red with fury and exertion, and this time he ducked his head when he came plowing in again.

A wild punch caught Rick high on the forehead, breaking the easy rhythm of his movements. Jackie saw the look of smug amusement leave his face, to be replaced by anger.

Ed caught him again, over the heart, before he could get his balance back, and then Rick backpedaled quickly, Ed hurrying after him.

Rick stopped moving and waited, flat-footed for the rush. He blocked Ed's wildly swinging fists, and his own left fist jolted out in a straight hard line, driving into Ed's midsection between his belt and the bottom of his ribs.

Ed stopped, poised as though on a diving board, leaning forward slightly, his mouth open and his arms folded across his body, his face suddenly gray.

Jackie stared at him, the protruding eyes, the open mouth and the gray face—she knew he wasn't breathing, that he couldn't breathe, and in sudden alarm she cried, "Rick!"

"Don't you worry, honey-girl," he said, smiling easily again. "He'll be ready for number two in just a minute."

And as he finished speaking there was the loud grating noise of Ed Warner dragging air into his lungs. His face went from gray to red, and he started to fold over even more, and Rick's right fist came up suddenly from his side and pounded into Ed's face, just under his left eye, and Ed fell over backwards onto the floor.

"Come on, Ed-boy," Rick said gently. "You aren't out. You're just a little tired, and you can't rest on Jackie's floor.

It's time for you to go home now." He leaned down and grabbed a handful of Ed's red hair and dragged Ed to his feet. Ed's eyes were glazed now—he seemed barely conscious of what was happening to him.

Rick held him upright, his hand still grasping hair, and his other hand, open and rigid, slapped fore and back across Ed's face, leaving white marks against the red. Ed started and shook his head.

Rick let him go. Ed stumbled but stayed upright. When he looked at Rick now it was clear that he recognized him, and equally clear that he hated him.

"Go on, Ed-boy," said Rick. "Before I have to show you number three. Go on, get going."

Without a word, Ed turned and walked to the door, weaving slightly as though he were half-drunk. His head hung forward, and his arms were limp at his sides. His shoulder hit the doorjamb as he was going through and he almost fell. Momentarily, he leaned into the door for support, then Jackie heard him going slowly and heavily down the stairs.

Rick crossed the room and shut the door. He came back then and helped Jackie to her feet. "You feel okay now?" he asked her.

"Better," she said. "Still shaky."

"You want a drink?"

"Please."

He led her to the sofa, sat her down, and went away. He came back a minute later with gin on the rocks, and she drank thirstily.

"Feel better?" he asked her. He hadn't joined her on the sofa, but was still standing in front of her.

She nodded. "Yes. Thank you. I'm glad you were here, Rick."

"Johnny on the spot," he agreed. "He really got mad at you out there, didn't he?"

She raised her head to look at him. "You could hear him out there?" she asked.

"The way he was shouting," Rick said, "you could have heard him clear to Youngstown."

Jackie looked up at him, frowning in confusion and suspicion. "Rick," she said, "why didn't you stop him out there? Why did you wait until he came in here?"

"Well," he said, and the same easy smile was on his face as when he'd been taunting Ed, "I wanted to talk to you about that, Jackie. And to tell you the truth, I didn't mind Ed's softening you up first, if you know what I mean."

"No," she said slowly, watching him, "I don't know what you mean, Rick. I don't know what you mean at all."

"I mean that you do need a protector," he said. "I wanted you to clearly understand that, to see the kind of position you're in, just a lone girl, all by yourself, and because you're selling it guys like Ed Warner think you're fair game. They can rough you up and give you a bad time all the way around, you see what I mean?"

"So far," she said. "What are you leading up to, Rick?"

"I want twenty per cent," he said calmly.

She'd seen it coming, from about five sentences back, but she'd expected him to ask for ten per cent, at the most. The size of the percentage he wanted from her stopped her for just a second. Then she shook her head and said, "No. Definitely not."

"Well, now, honey-girl," he said, with the easy smile still on his face, "I guess I haven't explained it all to you yet. Once I explain it to you, I think you'll see where I'm right. Twenty per cent is dirt cheap. Stand up, will you?"

She felt the twinge of fear returning. "What?"

"Stand up, honey-girl," he said. "I feel like standing, and I think it would be a lot easier to talk if we were both on the same level, so you just stand up now, okay?"

The way he said it, she knew better than to argue. She stood up, carefully, surprised to discover that her legs would hold her, and stared at Rick with sullen defiance.

"Now," he said, "here's the situation. I thought of this idea to begin with, am I right? I'm the guy, I mean, who dreamed the whole thing up from the outset."

"All right," she said. "I know that."

"Okay," he said. "Fine. Now, in the second place, I'm the guy who spread the word among the guys in the dorms, am I right? Even if you'd thought up the idea yourself—which you didn't—you still needed some guy to do your advertising for you in the dorms. That guy was me. Are you with me so far, honey-girl?"

"I'm with you," she said sullenly.

"Fine," he said. "I'm glad to hear it. Now comes the most important part. Ed Warner. He was the first, but he won't be the last."

"You're the second," she said.

He laughed, cocking his head to one side so the ridge showed on the side of his neck. "Right you are, honey-girl," he said. "I'm the second. And I *will* be the last. Put it this way, Jackie-girl. You are knocking down a hell of a lot of loot. There are a lot of hungry guys around this campus who could get the same idea Ed Warner had—knock it out of you—or the same idea I've got—go into partnership with you. Now, *somebody* is going to be your partner, honey-girl, and there just aren't any two ways about it. You can't run this thing without a protector, without somebody around to see to it you don't get beat up or robbed or blackmailed or anything else. You're going to have to have somebody around."

"No, I'm not," she said.

His smile didn't falter as his right hand swung up and around and cracked against the side of her face. "Don't interrupt me, honey-girl," he said pleasantly. "And don't contradict me. Now, as I said, you're going to have to have somebody around, some guy to see to it that all the other wolves keep off your back. And what would be fairer than to give that job to the guy who thought this racket up for you in the first place and found you all your customers?"

"I don't need you anymore," she said savagely. The side of her face burned where he had hit her, but for some reason she was no longer afraid of him. She was only blazingly angry. "You've done all you can for me," she snapped. "I've got the idea now, and I've got the customers, and I don't need you around anymore."

"Oh, but you do, honey-girl," he said softly. "You really do. And I'll tell you why. Because there are a lot of sadists in the world, a lot of sex perverts, and a lot of crooks who'll just be out for your money. One of them is liable to show up any time at all, and when he shows up this is what he's going to do."

His fist suddenly drove out, in the same kind of punch he had first used on Ed Warner, pounding into her in the same spot, just above the waist. Pain lanced up and out from the point of contact—a burning pain that shriveled through her lungs and cauterized her throat and stopped her breathing, a knifing pain that sliced down through her abdomen to her groin and cut off the blood in her legs and left her standing hunched and open-mouthed, a mummy, unbreathing, filled with pain.

Through the roaring of the pain, she could hear him talking again, his voice still pleasant, his smile still easy, his eyes as cold as space. "And that would be just the beginning of it, honey-girl," he was saying. "If it was one of these sadists or one of these sex perverts, that would be just the beginning of it."

Her throat opened, and when she dragged air into her straining lungs, it was a fresh pain. The air pulled screaming agony into her throat and down into her lungs, just as his fist lashed out again. This time he hit her on the tip of the left breast with such force that she was driven backward into the wall, and the pain in her breast was so terrible that she knew she just couldn't stand it. She opened her mouth to scream, but his hand, cold and heavy, clapped across her mouth before the scream ever got out, and he was saying, "A sadist or a sex pervert, honey-girl, he'd know a lot better than to let you scream. And he wouldn't be done yet, either." His knee shot up into her groin, his hand left her mouth, and he punched her twice in the stomach, then stepped quickly back so that when she doubled over and vomited none of it hit him.

She fell to her knees in her own sickness, and vomited again while Rick went over to the sofa, sat down, lit a cigarette and waited, glancing through her General Science textbook. "I took this when I was a freshman, you know?" he said conversationally. "Maybe you were smart to wait till now. You know you can't go to the cops or anybody. This is just between you and me."

She didn't know how long he sat there, while she lay unable to move on the floor, but finally he got up again and walked over to her. She was lying on the floor so that all she could see were his brown loafers and the bottom of his khaki pants. He said, "Twenty per cent, honey-girl?"

She managed to get the word out, though it tore her throat. "Yes."

3

PROFESSOR BLAKE was mumbling about Marlowe, and most of the class was asleep with its eyes open. It was the day after the beating, Friday, and Jackie was still sore, particularly since she'd had three appointments last night and all three customers had shown up. She had been amazed to discover that Rick's beating hadn't left a mark on her body.

She had never really known Rick. That was obvious. She had never really known anything about Rick Marshall, who or what he was. That beating hadn't been the work of an amateur. To inflict so much pain in so short a time and not leave a single mark on her body—that was the work of someone who had had practice.

And he had done it without ever raising his voice or even acting angry! When she thought back on it, that was the most frightening part. He hadn't even been angry, as Ed Warner had been. He had simply been educating her, calmly and efficiently and unemotionally. Unemotionally, that had been it, that had been the most terrifying part of it. He had done all that to her, beaten her that badly, and had shown absolutely no emotion while he was doing it, neither rage nor pleasure.

How could anybody be like that? It was like one of those science-fiction horror movies, when the hero is attacked by a robot or something, cold and unemotional and totally *un-reachable*. There was no plea, no mercy, no escape possible.

After he had left, yesterday afternoon, she had dragged herself to the shower, turned the water on while she was fully dressed, and only slowly did the cold water revive her enough to enable her to strip off the filthy, odorous clothes. Then she had cleaned the living room floor—only a touch of it had landed on the rug, most of it was on the wooden flooring—and then she had gone to the bedroom and collapsed on the bed. She hadn't awakened until her first customer had knocked on the door at nine o'clock.

She got up stiff and sore in every joint of her body. It had been a strain to smile at the eager boy who had dashed into the room when she unlocked the door for him. It had been a strain to act as though his eager thrashings on the bed were pleasurable to her when, in actuality, all they did was bring back the biting reminders of the pain that Rick had caused.

And when the ten o'clock boy had fondled her left breast, she hadn't been able to completely stifle the small scream that formed in her throat. The boy had been properly contrite and naturally curious, but Jackie's first blurted excuse, that she had walked into a door, had satisfied him. The boy had laughed over that and said, "Yeah, I guess that would land first, wouldn't it? Now me, I'd of hit my nose. What about this one?" And Jackie had assured him that the right breast was fine.

She thought midnight would never come, and when the third boy had been sent home satisfied and she had finally been able to fall asleep again, she had slept until almost noon, missing all her morning classes.

When she did wake up, just before twelve, she was still stiff and aching, but there were two changes. First, she had finally come to accept the inevibility of Rick's twenty per cent. And second, she had figured out how to get the money back.

She would take on a *female* partner.

That was going to be necessary anyway. Already, in only three weeks, her clientele had grown to the point where she had had to turn customers away. She only had two open hours left next week, and they would undoubtedly be booked this afternoon, after Blake had finished his droning on Marlowe for this week.

A second girl, that was the answer. And that second girl would stay with Jackie in her apartment. She'd be working for her. Rick would undoubtedly demand the same twenty per cent from her, and Jackie would want twenty per cent as well, which would leave the girl sixty per cent of her earnings. But sixty per cent of a full week's work, at ten dollars a trick, was still ninety dollars, and to a lot of girls ninety dollars a week was an awful lot of money.

But which girl should it be? Eating breakfast, driving out to the campus to attend this one class today, she had gone over and over the list of girls she knew in the college, trying to decide which one of them to approach. She couldn't afford to take any chances. She couldn't afford to approach a girl who would say no. If the girl said no and didn't become involved, there would be no way to force her to keep quiet.

She might go straight to Dean Kelland, or she might just tell one or two other girls in the dorm, but sooner or later the whole story would be out.

She didn't narrow it down to Rita Amherst until she was in class, with Blake droning on and Rita sitting across the way, on the other side of the discussion table.

Rita Amherst was short and well-built, but a bit on the plump side, with large ripe breasts and round soft hips and a waist not quite narrow enough. Her face was well-featured and, without her habitual look of discontent, it would have been very pretty. Her hair was black, chopped short in an Italian cut, and she didn't know the first thing about cosmetics.

There was nothing to worry about as far as appearance went. Steady money—and steady sex, too, probably—would undoubtedly remove that expression of discontent and let Rita's face be pretty. The hair was fine as it was, and Jackie could teach her how to use make-up properly. Perhaps she could take Rita on a few shopping trips for new clothes.

That took care of the physical side. The mental side was a bit more complicated. Rita was a poor girl, from a mining family, in college on a scholarship and working like mad nights at the Three Brothers Restaurant in town. She had made it plain often enough in the last two years—she, too, was a junior, twenty years old—that she envied Jackie for her money, her apartment, her car, her clothes, her poise and her freedom. Rita, of course, lived in the dorm, where she had to be present and accounted for by eleven p.m. week nights and one a.m. on weekends.

Rita was envious; she wanted money and freedom. But did she want it badly enough? Jackie had no idea what Rita's sex life was like, but she assumed that Rita was at that stage of discontented frustration and desperation where it no longer really mattered what her sex life or her convictions on sex might be. At any rate, she could sound the girl out, cautiously at first, and if it didn't look right, she'd be able to stop and change the subject before Rita learned anything dangerous.

The time passed slowly, Blake droning on like a drowsy midsummer fly, and all at once it was ten minutes to two, the class was over, and the students were all awake again.

Throughout the hour, Jackie had ignored Rick Marshall, sitting to her right in the next chair. She had to pay him his twenty per cent, that was clear enough, but she didn't have to talk to him. As the class was dismissed, he started to say something to her, the usual easy smile on his face, but she turned her back on him and walked quickly across the room to Rita Amherst. "Rita," she said, "I want to talk to you about something, but I'm going to be tied up until three o'clock. Could I meet you in the library then? Or maybe a few minutes later?"

Rita looked confused but pleased. To have Jackie Hayes—wealthy, slender, popular and usually so aloof—seek her out this way, ask to meet Rita Amherst, specifically— almost like making an appointment with her—was surprising and gratifying. She betrayed her embarrassed confusion by a slight blush, and by stammering through her, "Sure, Jackie. I'd be glad to—sure. Three o'clock."

"Five after three at the latest," Jackie told her.

"I'll be there," Rita assured her happily, and then Bob Silver, who'd been hanging around Rita lately, came along and said hello to Jackie and moved Rita away.

Jackie stood looking after them for a moment, knowing that Rita wouldn't be any trouble at all but that Bob Silver might be a good deal of trouble. She didn't know Bob very well, but being interested in Rita he would almost have to be trouble one way or the other. Either by wanting to horn in on the profits, like Rick, or by refusing to let Rita come into the business, all depending on his point of view.

Well, she could cross that bridge when she came to it. So far as she knew, Rita and Bob weren't going steady yet, so maybe there wouldn't be any trouble at all. And if trouble came, well, that was what Rick was getting his twenty per cent for.

Thinking of Rick, she glanced around the classroom to see if he was still there, but the room had now emptied, except for Professor Blake, who was still stuffing notes and textbooks into a thick brief case. She nodded to him. He looked uncomfortable. He was still thinking about that doodle, she realized. She went off for her appointment hour.

The next week's two open hours were filled in the first ten minutes. During the rest of the hour eight more boys came along, wanting appointments for next week. She'd had to tell them she was completely dated up. But she suggested they try again on Monday, since there was a good chance that there would be another girl coming into the business. Three of them asked, "As good as you, Jackie?" and she smiled and answered, "Better."

At five to three, Rick came by. He settled in the chair across the table from her, and grinned lazily. "How are you today, honey-girl?" he asked her.

"Sore," she said, controlling her anger.

He shrugged. "I guess we won't have to go through anything like that again, will we?"

"No."

"You're being a good girl," he said approvingly. "So I'll give you a break. The twenty per cent won't be retroactive, the way I figured at first. No, it'll start as of next Monday. How's that?"

"Fine," she said.

He nodded and grinned some more. "By the way," he said, "that's a shrewd idea you've got."

"Which idea is that?"

"Rita Amherst." The grin broadened. "You didn't figure to keep me from knowing, did you?"

"No," she said.

"I mean, you know I'll have to have twenty per cent of her dough, too, isn't that right?"

"I suppose so," she said. "I thought you'd probably want it."

"Well, you know how it is, honey-girl," he said. "Going to college is an expensive proposition these days."

"I know," she said.

"Three o'clock you'll talk to her, huh? In the library." He smiled. "Talk in the biology section," he said. "Maybe it'll inspire her." Languidly he got to his feet. "And bring her around to the apartment when you're done convincing her," he said. "I'll want to talk to her myself a bit." He nodded and went away. He had his own key to the apartment, had had it made back in the very beginning, three weeks ago.

Jackie looked after him, hating him and knowing her own helplessness before him, until he had weaved lithely through the tables of the Student Union and out the far door. Then she glanced up at the clock. Just three. Time for her meeting with Rita.

Rita was in the library, waiting by the main desk, which was just about the worst spot she could have picked. "Hi," said Jackie quickly. "Let's go some place where we can talk without disturbing anybody."

"Sure," said Rita. Curiosity and pleasure were plain in her eyes.

Way in the back of the library were record-listening rooms, small enclosed booths lined with soundproofing, each containing one record player and two chairs. Theoretically, smoking wasn't allowed in the library, but the authorities had long since given up, and an ash tray was on the table beside the record player, directly under the NO SMOKING sign.

Jackie lit a cigarette and offered Rita one, which Rita stammeringly refused. "I wanted to talk to you about something important," she began, "but I want to lead up to it slowly." Now, at the moment of procuring, Jackie felt herself developing a very bad case of stage-fright. She kept it held in, controlled, beneath the surface, and outwardly she was calm and pleasant, smoking a cigarette and chatting in a quiet, friendly voice.

At Jackie's pause, after this opening, Rita nodded and said, "Sure, Jackie."

"First I want to talk about me," Jackie told her, "and then I want to talk about you, and then I have a—" the word 'proposition' occurred to her, but she rejected it "—an offer to make you. But I don't want to rush things. You do have some time, haven't you?"

At the mention of time, Rita automatically looked at her left wrist, which was bare, and then nodded in confusion. "Oh, sure, Jackie."

"What happened to your watch? Being fixed?"

Rita's confusion increased and she said, "Yes. Uh—well, no. Uh, you see, I had to pawn it. Uh, my father—well, I ran a little short of money and uh—" She shrugged, spreading her hands, an expression of obvious appeal on her face, begging Jackie to say something, to fill the silence and not leave Rita just sitting there.

"Well, that's part of what I want to talk to you about," said Jackie, thinking, *Better and better.* "Now, I don't know how to say this. Maybe just straightforward and frank."

"Oh, sure, Jackie."

"Well, I have money, you know? I mean, I have my own car, and lots of clothes, and I have my own apartment off-campus, and all of that."

"I know," said Rita, nodding. Her face was serious now. She looked more bewildered than ever, as though she couldn't believe that Jackie had brought her here just to flaunt her own wealth in front of her.

"Your family's poor, isn't it?" said Jackie softly, and her face shone with friendly sympathy.

Rita looked down at her hands, curling in her lap. She shrugged, nervously, and said, her voice so low Jackie could barely hear it, "I suppose so."

"I'll tell you a secret," said Jackie, and when Rita looked up Jackie was smiling as though they both already shared the secret. "My family's poor, too," she said. "A lot poorer than yours." She held a hand up to stop Rita's words of amazed disbelief, and said, "My father was a banker, did you know that? Well, the mill in town moved south. It was practically the only support for the town, so the bank folded, and my father has all kinds of debts, and now our family is as poor as yours, and even more so." That, she reflected, was a lot quicker and simpler than the truth.

Rita's face now showed innocent concern. "I didn't know about that, Jackie," she said.

"Nobody knows about it," Jackie told her. "It happened a couple of months ago. But I've still got plenty of money, and I've still got my car, and I've still got my apartment, and I still buy all the clothes I want."

Jackie paused, and the silence lengthened, until Rita finally became aware that some comment was expected of her. She said what Jackie had wanted her to say. "Well, how in the world do you do anything like that?"

"That's what I want to tell you about, Rita," Jackie said. "How I can have all this money—eighty or ninety dollars a week sometimes—even though my family is probably even poorer than yours. And how you could make that much money, too."

Rita was alert now, and eager. Jackie went on, treading cautiously. "It's a secret, though," she said. "Not many people know about it. I'd want to be sure you were interested before I told you what it was."

"Oh, I'm interested," Rita said promptly. Her eyes had brightened, the beginning of a smile lingered at the corners of her mouth. She was sitting up much straighter in the chair.

Jackie stubbed her cigarette out in the ash tray and lit another one. This time, when she offered one to Rita, Rita accepted. "The thing is," said Jackie, "it's kind of illegal, what

I'm doing. Nothing really bad, nothing like stealing or anything like that. I mean, I wouldn't be sent to jail or anything
if I were caught, but I'd probably be thrown out of school,
that's all. That's why I have to be so careful, before I tell you
what it is. Would that bother you, if it were illegal?"

Doubt crossed Rita's face, and hesitantly she asked, "It
isn't stealing? Or selling dope or anything like that?"

Jackie shook her head. "Nothing like that at all." She
smiled. "It's work, kind of. But it's easy work, just a few
hours a day, and you can make eighty or ninety dollars a
week. And of course you'd have to live off-campus, in my
apartment with me."

"Off-campus? But I couldn't do that. I have to live in the
dorm."

"Don't you worry about it," Jackie told her. "We'll fix it
for you the same way I fixed it for me. Now, Rick and I
are—"

"Rick? You mean Rick Marshall?"

"Sure."

"Is he part of this?"

Jackie nodded, a bit confused herself now at Rita's sudden questioning.

Rita smiled and shook her head. "Gee," she said, "how
silly can you get? Until you said Rick was part of it, I
thought—I mean, after you said I'd have to live at your
apartment with you—" Her voice petered off and she smiled
again.

Jackie was alert again, hoping she was catching the drift
right. "What did you think?" she asked quickly.

"Well—but it's silly, I don't know, I—you know, you said
it was illegal and—"

"Well, go on," said Jackie, smiling encouragement. "What did you think it was?"

"Well," said Rita, "I almost thought you meant—uh—prostitution."

Jackie smiled with the other girl and said, as though she were continuing a joke, "What if it were prostitution? What if that had been what I had in mind? I mean, just suppose. What would you have said?"

Rita was suddenly confused again, her hands making small motions in her lap while she searched for words. "Well, uh, I don't know. I mean, a little town like Clifton—"

I've got her, Jackie thought. *She's hooked.* Her smile broadened and she said, "Because that's what it is."

"I mean—What?" Rita's eyes had opened wide, they seemed to fill her face, and her expression was comically astounded.

"That's just what it is, Rita," Jackie said calmly, and she kept on talking, rapidly but softly, persuasively, keeping up a steady stream of talk that would keep Rita from thinking too much before she got used to the idea. "When it happened, the bank failing, two months ago—" it was only three weeks, but she thought it would be better if Rita had the idea this had been going on for a long time already "—I told Rick about it, and how I was going to have to leave school, and how sick and worried I was about the whole thing. We'd been going to bed together, you know how it is, and he said, kind of half-kidding, 'Don't give it away for free any more,' and I thought about it, and I realized it was the only way I could stay in school and still have all the money I needed. I mean, nobody gets hurt or anything, and it hasn't ruined my reputation or anything like that. The boys know I need the money, and they know I'll give them a good time, and we're all friends."

"But," Rita broke in, "but to be a—to—*prostitution,* Jackie."

"Oh, come on, Rita, what's the difference, really? A boy takes you out on a date and he spends ten dollars for movies and drinks and dinner and everything else, and all he's doing is trying to get you into the mood to go to bed with him. And if you do, that's what he's spent his ten dollars for. And if you don't, then he's spent his ten dollars and he's been cheated. This is just the same thing, except that instead of the money going to movie owners and restaurant owners and bartenders, it goes to me. Isn't it better that way?

"Besides the boy knows there isn't any chance that he'll be wasting the ten dollars. And instead of having to do it all cramped up on a back seat of a car somewhere, here's a nice clean apartment and a bed, and they've got a whole hour to spend with me. It's an easy way to make money, and nobody gets hurt or anything. And we can't get caught, because if any of the boys told, they'd be in trouble, too."

Rita, by this time, was looking interested in spite of herself, though there were still frown wrinkles on her forehead, and she still kept saying, "But—" every time Jackie stopped for breath. But she hadn't yet said "No" and she hadn't yet stood up and walked out. She was hooked, and all Jackie had to do was keep talking to her.

So that's what she did. She told her the money arrangement, that she would get two dollars of every ten Rita made—"to pay the apartment rent and for supplies and like that"—and Rick would get another two dollars—"because we need a man around to protect us from anybody who'd want to steal from us or blackmail us or anything like that"—and Rita would get the remaining six, which meant ninety dollars a week. "Ninety dollars," she concluded, "for fifteen hours' work a week, and it really couldn't be called work. It's more like fun, if you know what I mean. You aren't a virgin, are you?"

"Yes," said Rita, and that was bad, but she said it regretfully, and that was good.

"Good heavens!" said Jackie, in mock astonishment. "Twenty years old and still a virgin? Well, good heavens, it's time you took care of that anyway! Don't you know what you've been missing?"

Rita laughed self-consciously and said, "I guess not."

"Well, we'll have Rick take care of that this afternoon," Jackie said, rapid and businesslike, as though they were discussing the filling out of a form rather than the loss of virginity. "The first time is the toughest for a boy, and we wouldn't want to make it too difficult for a paying customer. And besides, Rick is awful good. He won't hurt you a bit."

Rita was blushing furiously by now and saying, "I don't know, Jackie, I don't know—"

Jackie wondered if she'd mentioned Rick too soon. But she was going to have to mention him, because Rick would want her first anyway, and Rita had to be handled more delicately than was Rick's style, at least until she had agreed and serviced a couple of customers. Then she'd be in with no way to get out again. Until then, she had to be handled delicately.

"It's an awful lot of money," she told Rita, "for doing practically nothing at all, and living in a nice apartment off-campus. And we'll get you some new clothes, and maybe later on a car. I mean, look at me, I've been doing it for two months now, and it certainly hasn't been bad for me, has it?"

"No, I guess it hasn't," admitted Rita.

"Then you'll come in with me?"

Rita gnawed her lower lip as she looked everywhere around the room but at Jackie. Finally, she nodded almost imperceptibly and said, "I could sure use the money."

"Fine," said Jackie, taking that for yes. She got to her feet. "Let's go see Rick."

Rick was waiting in the living room when they arrived. He smiled and said, "Hi, Rita. You one of the happy family now?"

"I guess so," said Rita and started blushing again.

Rick patted the sofa beside him. "Come on and sit down," he said. "I guess Jackie told you about everything— the money breakdown and all that."

"Uh-huh," said Rita. She sat beside him, looking at Rick with bright and frightened, but excited, eyes. *She knows she's going to sleep with him,* Jackie thought, *and she's looking forward to it. And Rick is smarter than I thought; he's going to give her the delicate treatment after all.*

Jackie sat in the chair across the room while Rick talked about football practice and about the game with Ypsilaw three weeks from now, which would be the big game of the season. He talked casually, as though idle talk was all they were there for, and Jackie saw that it was working, that Rita was losing her tenseness, and that when Rick casually put his arm around her she moved against him willingly enough. Whenever Rita glanced her way, she smiled encouragingly, and she wondered when would be the best moment to slip away.

When Rick finally turned his head and kissed Rita, Jackie got to her feet. It was a long kiss and Jackie saw that Rita, after the first hesitation, responded fully and warmly. Jackie waited, standing, for the kiss to be finished. Then she would make some excuse and leave the room.

But when Rick saw her standing there, he smiled and said, "Sit down, Jackie. No need to rush off. We're all friends here. And besides, Rita is liable to teach you something, aren't you, Rita?" And he laughed and squeezed Rita closer.

Rita looked worried again, a bit frightened, and she murmured, "I—I'm a virgin."

"Well, don't you worry about that," Rick said, and he kissed her again, motioning angrily behind Rita's back for Jackie to sit down.

Jackie did so, trying to keep her expression blank. *That clever bastard,* she thought, *that clever bastard.* Making Rita with somebody watching, because that way, with Jackie sitting right there, Rita wouldn't have the guts to back out at the last minute—because that way there'd be just one more reason for her never telling anybody what was going on in this apartment. And also, Jackie knew, Rick wanted her around because he wanted to excite her, he wanted Jackie to get all hot and bothered, watching another couple making love.

Rick was now murmuring in Rita's ear, talking soothingly to her, kissing her mouth and throat and ears, his hands roaming gently on her body. Rita's eyes kept closing in catlike sensuality when he stroked her. She looked less and less often over at Jackie, who kept smiling encouragingly, and Jackie thought, *That clever bastard. He's better than I thought. He's making her forget I'm here. He's really doing it, making her forget I'm here.*

She watched, fascinated in spite of herself, while Rick, across the room, slowly went through the careful steps of seduction—murmuring, kissing, fondling, slowly stripping the clothes away until they were nude together. *And Rita,* Jackie thought, *has forgotten me completely; forgotten me and every-body and everything except the touch of Rick.*

But when they came together, white and white together on the darkness of the sofa, and Rick with one quick thrust stole her virginity, Rita cried out and her eyes opened wide and her head turned until she was staring with terror at Jackie. Jackie hastily put the smile on her face again and nod-ded, her hands clenching in her lap. *He didn't have to do this to me,* she was thinking, *he didn't have to do this to me. It wasn't neces-sary.*

Then Rita shuddered and her eyes snapped shut, her arms clamped around Rick's back, and her body drove up-ward to meet him. The only sound in the room was their breathing.

It's stupid anyway, Jackie was thinking, *it isn't exciting at all, to watch this way. They look ridiculous.*

She closed her eyes and tried to think of other things. *We'll put a bed in the dining room,* she thought, *make that Rita's bedroom. And tomorrow we'll see about the relative letters, so she can move off-campus.*

But despite herself her eyes opened, and despite herself she watched. She watched Rita's passion-contorted face, her writhing body, and despite herself the thoughts came to her.

But they weren't the thoughts Rick was expecting.

I wish I were a man, she was thinking. *I wish I could do that to Rita. I wish I were a man.*

4

MOVING DAY was a mess, but they had no choice. With five of them working now, the old apartment was far too small. So they'd rented a house, using Sandy McGowan's name. The landlord had written the appropriate note to Dean Kelland saying that he was Sandy's uncle. Jackie was keeping the old apartment, but only to live in and for personal reasons. The Maple Street house was now their base of operations.

All in all, the Maple Street house was perfect, even better than the old apartment had been. Once again, it was on a corner, and this time it was flanked by a vacant lot on the other side, a lot that extended halfway down the block before there was another house. And directly across the street was a Roman Catholic church, a large church—for a town the size of Clifton—with sprawling grounds surrounding it.

And they had the whole house to themselves. On the ground floor, a large living room, a medium-sized dining room and a medium-sized kitchen, plus a fourth room which could be a den or a sewing room or whatever you wanted, depending on who you were. It was now going to be a bedroom.

There were four more bedrooms on the second floor and—wonder of wonders—two bathrooms, each one with doors leading to two bedrooms, so that one could get directly to a bathroom from any of the four bedrooms.

The place had come completely furnished, with an extra fifth bed in the unfinished attic, which was immediately moved down to the first-floor bedroom. This bedroom was Jackie's, and Rita lettered carefully four small cards which were thumb-tacked to the doors of the four upstairs bedrooms: "Rita" "Sandy" "Laura" and "Honey".

In the three weeks, since Jackie had talked Rita into coming to work for her, a lot had happened. November had become December, and the streets were now slush-covered, the wide lot to the left of the house blanketed in white snow, crisscrossed with the trails of dogs and small boys. Jackie's clientele had grown steadily. Rita, almost from the very beginning, worked fifteen hours a week, making a full ninety dollars. She had been shy and terribly embarrassed at first, but that had worn off and for a week or two she had seemed to be enjoying herself hugely. She was happier, prettier, and certainly wealthier.

But the demand once again went beyond the supply, so Jackie had gone talent-hunting again, this time coming back with Laura Rance. Laura was a tall and slender girl, built much like Jackie, but her hair was black and straight, and her face was a long serious oval. She was the only girl political science major in school, and she spent all her hours, when not either in class or in bed, reading huge, dim tomes with improbable titles. She wore glasses, except when working, and had very little to say. She was attending school on a scholarship, having been raised in an orphanage outside Cleveland. Jackie had used much the same tactics in procuring her as she had used with Rita, except that Laura had caught on much faster, had agreed at once, and had spent a long while arguing about money before Rick convinced her, through almost unstated threats of violence, not to fight the status quo.

Once Laura had joined the group—they were still in the old apartment at that time—Rita had changed again, becoming somewhat sullen and ill at ease. Jackie correctly diagnosed her complaint as jealousy. She knew that Rita had enjoyed living with Jackie, being the only girl who shared Jackie's secret and Jackie's occupation.

And Rita's disposition wasn't improved when girls number four and five were added to the menagerie. Jackie had gone out after number four—Honey Bane—because the clientele was still on the increase. There were eighteen hundred students at Clifton College, and somewhat more than half of these—about a thousand—were boys. And the word had been spreading like wildfire in the male dorms.

Honey Bane was a soft, warm, baby-faced blonde who, Jackie suspected, had a mild case of nymphomania. She was, at any rate, the only one of the five who went out on a busman's holiday every Saturday and Sunday night, with various of her favorite customers. Four days a month, Honey was miserable, snappish as a cat, prowling the house and chewing on her lower lip. The rest of the time she was happy as a lark—in mating season.

At the same time that Jackie brought Honey Bane into the fold, Rick showed up with Sandy McGowan. It seemed that Sandy had already been supporting herself in this way, but in a much less organized manner. She had been living in the dormitory, working without a base, using handy woods or automobile back seats for the plying of her trade. She had also restricted her clientele to a very few boys whom she knew and trusted, and she had only been charging five dollars. She was delighted at the prospect of getting a dollar more per trick, of having her own bed in her own room in which to ply her trade, and of no longer having to live in a dormitory on campus.

Sandy was red-haired, pale-skinned and green-eyed, with a Playboy Playmate figure and a coolly beautiful face. She was quiet and reserved, and she kept a locked metal box under her bed, where she stored her savings.

All of the girls, with the exception of Rita, were happy with their lives. Laura was still annoyed by the forty per cent of her income sliced off the top by Jackie and Rick, Honey was still annoyed at the monthly vacation she was forced to take, and Sandy was annoyed whenever she had an uncustomered hour while one or more of the other girls was working, but aside from this they all got along very well with one another.

Moving day was a Saturday, for it wouldn't interrupt business and they would have a day of rest after moving. They had no furniture to take with them, only clothing and personal possessions, but it was still a madly chaotic day. Though they started at ten in the morning, it was after seven that evening before they were in the Maple Street house and completely squared away. Rick then made drinks and all of them except Rita sat around the living room of their new house and relaxed, toasting one another and wishing for continued success.

Jackie asked Rita to join the rest of them, but she refused sullenly and stayed in her room, lying on the bed fully dressed, with the lights off, until long after the rest had gone to sleep that night. The others slept alone—even Honey was too worn out by the day's moving to think about going out for a man—with the exception of Sandy. Rick stayed over that night and, as had become his habit, he stayed with Sandy. *He's trying to make me jealous,* Jackie thought. *The damn fool is trying to make me jealous, and he doesn't even know that there's only one person in this whole house that I want to go to bed with, and that one person isn't him.*

She pushed that thought immediately out of her mind again, but the memory of it lingered. She was *not* in love with Rita Amherst. She had simply been affected, embarrassed, made to feel awkward and strange, by watching Rick seduce her that afternoon.

Then why, she asked herself, *do I keep Rita on? Rita isn't happy here, she doesn't like to be here, her conscience is hitting her pretty strongly now that the other girls are here and this is so obviously a business and not just for fun. If I didn't keep begging and insisting and convincing her to stay, she would leave in a flash. If I'm not in love with her, why do I want her to stay here?*

She told herself that she was afraid that Rita, once she had left, might talk to the wrong people, but even as she thought this she knew it wasn't so. It *is* so, she insisted to herself desperately. And the thought came, unbidden: *If it's so, then why is it I watch her sometimes, through the keyhole, when she's with a customer? Why is it I watch her, always her, not the boy? Why*

*is it I find myself wishing I were a man, just long enough to make love
to Rita Amherst?*

It took her a long while to get to sleep that night, as had
been happening a lot lately. And the weekends were always
the worst.

Monday evening, around six-thirty, Ed Warner came by.
Honey answered the door when the bell rang and she didn't
know better than to let him in. Jackie came in from the
kitchen where she'd been eating dinner, and Ed immediately
started to shout. "I've got the goddamn letter you wanted!"
he shouted. He was waving a business-size envelope above
his head, and he seemed furious and nervous. "Here's the
goddamn letter!" And he threw it at her.

Jackie looked at it. It was the most obvious forgery she
had ever seen. It had been done on a small portable typewriter, with bad erasures and strike-overs and typographical
errors, and it wasn't even on doctor's letterhead stationery,
just on a blank sheet of typewriter paper. It stated to whom-
ever might be concerned that Ed Warner no longer had the
disease he had brought back with him from Mexico.

Jackie handed the letter back, after noticing that the
name of the doctor had been written by someone amateur-
ishly trying to disguise his normal handwriting, and said,
"Come on, Ed. I'm not as stupid as all that. You wrote that
letter yourself."

"Who says so?" Ed shouted. His face was getting as red
as his hair, and his fists were clenched at his sides. "You calling me a liar?"

"Yes," Jackie told him. "And a bad one at that."

"I'm a customer!" he shouted. "I've got a goddamn right
to be a customer!"

"Not here," Jackie told him firmly. She glanced behind her, but the doorway was empty. Rick was back in the kitchen. She wondered if he was going to wait again for her to be half-beaten before coming to the rescue.

"What's the matter with him?" Honey asked innocently, her eyes roaming over Ed's body. "Can't he be a customer?"

"Not if you want to pass your blood test," Jackie told her.

"Oh, dear," said Honey. Her face paled, and she backed hastily away from Ed.

"I'm cured, goddamn it!" cried Ed. "That letter says so!"

His shouting had disrupted the whole household. Laura came downstairs to see what was going on. Sandy strolled in for the same purpose from the kitchen, where she had been having supper with Jackie and Rick. "What's all the shouting about?" Sandy wanted to know, and Laura said, "Maybe you don't know it, you people, but I'm upstairs trying to study."

Honey and Sandy were both wearing only bathrobes, Laura was unconcernedly garbed in bra and panties, and Jackie was dressed in toreador pants and a black sweater. All of this femininity around him—and all of it refusing him, and him alone—threw Ed into an even more furious rage than before. "You wanted the goddamn letter!" he screamed. "Now you've got it and here—" he fumbled for his wallet, so furious he couldn't control his movements. The wallet fell on the floor. He swooped down after it, then reached into it "—and here's the goddamn money!" He held up a thin stack of bills, and Jackie could see they were practically all tens. He glared from face to face. "Who wants it?" he demanded. "Come on, come on, you've got the lousy letter, who wants the money?"

"Rick is here," Jackie told him quietly. "In the kitchen."

"I don't care," screamed Ed. "I'm a goddamn customer."

Rick, from the doorway, said, "No, you're not, Ed. I thought we went through all this once before." Now that his name had been mentioned, he finally put in his appearance.

"I've got the letter!" screamed Ed, waving it above his head.

Rick took one step forward into the room. "Get out of here, Ed," he said.

Ed hesitated, looking from face to face. Sandy watched him coolly, Laura interestedly, Honey apprehensively, Jackie angrily and Rick insolently. Ed looked at them all, then backed reluctantly toward the door. "You'll get yours," he told them angrily. "All of you."

"Keep it cool, boy," Rick told him. "Remember what I told you last time—what would happen to you if you talked in the wrong places."

Ed glared and spat on the floor, then dashed from the house, slamming the door.

In the sudden silence, Laura said, with calm interest, "What's the matter with him, anyway? I mean, what've we got against him?"

"He went to Mexico last summer," Rick told her, "and he brought back a little something with him, and I don't mean a serape."

"Oh," said Laura.

"Oh, dear," said Honey again, just as terrified as the first time. Jackie couldn't understand why Honey had been as afraid as all that, but later on she found out. Honey didn't know very much about diseases of that type, and she had the wrong idea that catching it would put her out of commission.

An hour and a half later that evening, just after eight o'clock, they had their second visitor. Bob Silver, who had been going out with Rita occasionally—not yet going steady—up until the time Rita had come to live with Jackie.

Jackie had taken every precaution to keep Bob from finding out what Rita was doing, since Rita said he was a very strait-laced type and might very well try to make trouble, with the silly idea that he was protecting Rita. Rita had broken with him, picking a fight as an excuse, and hadn't seen him since. And Jackie had warned all of her customers not to tell Bob Silver anything about Jackie or Rita or any of the other girls. Up until now, everyone had kept quiet.

Jackie answered the bell the second time, wondering what customer was impatient enough to come an hour early, and when she opened the door and saw Bob Silver she knew exactly what had happened. This was Ed Warner's revenge. He must have gone straight to Bob after he left there, told Bob what Rita was doing these days, and left it for Bob to make all the trouble.

And it was obvious that Bob was ready to make as much trouble as he possibly could. His face was pale and tight as he said, "I want to talk to Rita, Jackie. I want to talk to her now."

Jackie felt her heart starting to pound, and she had a terrible feeling of inadequacy in this situation, but she managed to force a friendly smile onto her face, and somehow she kept her voice friendly and even as she said, "Well, sure, Bob. Come on in. I think Rita's upstairs. Come on into the living room. Sit down anywhere—that chair's about the best, you know these furnished apartments—I'll go on up and tell Rita you're here."

He didn't answer, and his tight pale expression didn't change as he came into the living room and sat down in the chair she had suggested. He sat there, rigid, waiting, watching Jackie with tightly controlled rage behind his eyes.

Jackie cleared her throat nervously, moved her hands aimlessly at her sides, and felt the smile slipping on her mouth. "I'll go on up," she said again, and fled upstairs.

Rita was, as usual these days, lying fully dressed on her bed, with no lights on in the room and the door closed. Jackie came in, flicked on the light, closed the door again behind her and, as Rita sat up blinking in the sudden glare, said, "Rita, we've got a little trouble downstairs. Bob Silver's here, and he says he wants to talk to you. From the look of him, he knows what's going on."

"Bob?" Rita had obviously been millions of miles away, thinking whatever private thoughts were hers these days, and it was taking her a few seconds to come back. "Bob?" she repeated. "Here? Downstairs?"

"Ed Warner must have told him," Jackie said. "To try to make trouble for us."

Rita was suddenly back. Her face drained of color and she leaped up from the bed. "Oh, no, Jackie!" she cried. "Bob will tell Dean Kelland and he'll tell the police. He's liable to even write to my parents or something—"

"Hold it, Rita, take it easy," Jackie said, speaking softly but rapidly. "We've got to figure out how to handle this. Do you think you can talk to him? Do you think you can act happy, smile and joke with him? Because if he thinks you aren't happy, he'll go straight to Dean Kelland and you can be *sure* he'll write letters to your parents and my parents and everybody else's parents."

"I don't know, Jackie," said Rita desperately, "I don't know."

"You've got to do it," Jackie told her. "Listen. Act surprised to see him, and pleased, too. Tell him you came here of your own free will—that I suggested it, but I didn't force you or anything—and that you're happy here and you have no intention of leaving here no matter what he says. Tell him it was the only way you could stay in school, that you'd pawned everything and your family couldn't afford to send you any more money and—Did you ever tell him about your family's money troubles?"

Rita nodded. Her eyes were wide, and the blood hadn't yet returned to her face.

"Fine," said Jackie. "So he'll know you're telling him the truth. Tell him it was the only way you could stay in school, and you'd lost your virginity two years ago anyway and—Hold on. Just sit there, don't go away, don't think, don't start crying, don't do anything. Just sit there for a second. I'll be right back."

Before Rita could answer, Jackie dashed across the hall and burst into Laura's room, where Laura was, as usual, studying. "You've got tranquilizers," Jackie said breathlessly. "Give me some."

"What's the matter this time?" Laura asked slowly.

"No time. I'll tell you later. Come on, come on, I've got to get back to Rita."

"All right, all right." Laura walked over to the bureau and opened the top drawer. "Maybe you ought to take one of these yourself," she said, handing the small bottle to Jackie.

"What's an overdose?" Jackie asked her.

"A what? Oh. You're not supposed to take more than two."

"What if you took three? Would it kill you?"

"No, but it would make you sleepy after a while. That's why they say to only—"

"How fast would it work?"

"Three of them? I don't know. Just a couple of minutes, I suppose."

"Fine." Jackie ran back across the hall, got a glass of water from the bathroom, and delivered glass and three pills to Rita. "Take these," she ordered, and Rita took them without a word. "They're Laura's tranquilizers," Jackie explained. "Now, you remember what I told you. You have to do this to stay in school, and it's your own free will, and you're happy here. And Rita, listen. Try to get him to come up here with you. Don't push that part too fast, but do your best. If you can get him to come up here with you, we'll be all right. I'll take your nine o'clock customer."

Since the staff had grown to five, and Jackie was making over a hundred dollars a week from her twenty per cent of the other girl's work alone, she no longer turned more than one trick a night herself, though she still made all the appointments, and now kept the books that were necessary.

"All right," said Rita.

"You wait up here a couple of minutes," Jackie told her, "until you feel those things taking effect. They're tranquilizers, they'll help you. I'll tell him you were taking a nap and you're getting dressed." She started toward the door, then turned back. "Can you remember everything?"

"I think so," said Rita, but there was still fright in her eyes.

"Do it for me, honey," said Jackie. "Do your best. It means a lot to all of us."

"I'll try," said Rita.

Jackie went back downstairs, pasted a smile on her face and said, "She was taking a nap, Bob. She has to get dressed. She'll be down in a minute."

Bob turned a bitter face to glare at Jackie. "You mean, she's with one of her *customers?*" he demanded.

"No," said Jackie easily. "We don't have any customers before nine o'clock."

He looked away from her and glared at the floor, a muscle twitching in his cheek, his right fist grinding into his left palm as he sat hunched forward, elbows on knees.

They waited together in the living room, in an uncomfortable silence, until Jackie heard a step on the stairs. She turned and said, "Ah, here she is now!" Out of the corner of her eye, she saw Bob leap to his feet, the bitterness on his face changing to a look of almost pathetic concern. She studied Rita, and saw that the tranquilizers had taken effect. The girl was smiling easily, coining gracefully down the stairs, and her, "Hi Bob. Long time no see," seemed as natural as breathing.

"I'll leave you two alone," said Jackie, and she retreated to the kitchen.

Rick was seated at the kitchen table, playing solitaire. He looked up when she came into the room, and nodded his head toward the front of the house. "What's going on out there?" he asked, his voice low.

Jackie kept her own voice down as she answered him. "Bob Silver's here. Ed Warner must have gone to him and told him about Rita after he left here."

"Bob? Now, what the hell are we going to do?"

"Rita's talking to him," Jackie said. "She's going to try to convince him to let things alone."

"Not Rita," said Rick positively. "You know that as well as I do. She's probably burst into tears already out there. She won't convince him of anything except that he should go straight to Dean Kelland."

"Maybe not. I gave her three of Laura's tranquilizers. I told her to try to take Bob upstairs with her. If she can work that, we'll be all right."

"She'll never do it," said Rick.

"Ssshh," said Jackie. She pressed her ear to the closed kitchen door and listened. She could hear the murmuring of voices, but she couldn't make out the words. "They're talking together," she reported. "They're being quiet about it. Rita isn't crying or anything."

"Not yet," said Rick pessimistically.

Jackie came over to the table. "All we can do is wait," she said. "And hope for the best."

"Want to play some gin rummy, while we wait for the ax to fall?"

"Why not?"

They played in silence for half an hour, then they heard the sound of movement from the living room. Jackie threw her cards down and ran across the room to peek through the keyhole in the kitchen door. The hall went straight through the house from kitchen door to front door, with the living room to the left, from Jackie's point of view, and the stairs on the right.

As she watched, Rita came into view, holding Bob's hand. She was smiling. He was looking dubious. Jackie watched, holding her breath, and saw the two of them start up the stairs. She straightened and turned, smiling crookedly at Rick. "She's done it," she said. "Our little girl has done it. They're on their way upstairs."

I should feel relieved, she thought. *I've won, I should feel relieved. Why is it I feel as though I've lost? I am not in love with Rita, that's stupid, I wish that thing had never happened when Rick made me watch, it's addled my brains, I should be feeling relieved.*

Rick grinned hugely and said, "Then that's that. I never thought Rita could do it."

"It isn't quite over with yet," Jackie reminded him. She felt brutal, she felt like lashing out at someone. "There's still Ed Warner. He's liable to try again."

"I'll take care of that matter right now," said Rick. He got to his feet. "I'll see you later on."

"All right."

He left and she sat down at the table and shuffled the cards, waiting for nine o'clock, when she would take over Rita's trick. Then she had one of her own at ten, and another one at eleven. This would be the first night she'd done all three tricks in weeks.

She shuffled the cards over and over, monotonously, and over and over and monotonously she repeated in her head: *I am not in love with Rita.*

Rick came back around one o'clock. He let himself in the back door, to which he had a key, and stood in the doorway of Jackie's bedroom. The knuckles on his left hand were skinned, but the familiar insolent smile was on his face and he held a self-conscious pose as he stood in the doorway. "Ed and I talked it over," he said, smiling. "He decided to leave school. Tomorrow. He figured that was the best thing all the way around."

"Fine," said Jackie.

"I'll be seeing you, honey-girl," said Rick, and he went on upstairs to Sandy.

The next afternoon, Rick came by with the suggestion for the party. He gathered the five girls together in the kitchen, sitting around the table, and began: "You know we're playing Anderson College this weekend. It's an away game, and it's the last game of the season. Right after the game is over a bunch of the guys on the team would like to break training in a great big way. They'd like to have themselves a little party, and they'd like you girls to come along and have the party with them after the game."

"Anderson's over three hundred miles from here," Jackie objected.

Rick held a hand up for silence. "Now, just hold on till I explain it," he said. "There's ten of us want to chip in on this thing. We'll pay for your transportation—maybe we can work it so we get you rides out there—and we'll pay the rent for wherever we hold the party. Besides that, we'll pay a hundred and fifty bucks to you girls, thirty bucks apiece, which is what you'd get for one night's work here. How does it sound?"

"Ten of you?" asked Jackie. "There's only five of us."

Rick shrugged. "Two guys for each girl. Nothing wrong with that, is there?" he asked, and his eyes were directly on Honey.

"Nothing at all," Honey replied huskily. "Not a thing."

"Sure," said Rick. "And what other problems are there? None."

"We keep all thirty this time," said Laura suddenly. "This is special, so we get to keep all of the money."

"Now, wait a second," said Rick. "I set this thing up. You're lucky I'm not asking for more than usual. What the hell, you'll get eighteen bucks out of it, a nice weekend outing, free tickets to a football game, and a good party, all thrown in. What the hell more do you want?"

"We keep the money," insisted Laura.

"Wait a second," said Sandy. "We're each going to have two customers, right? So we'll give Rick his two dollars per customer. Four dollars from each of us. But it isn't going to be here in this house, so Jackie doesn't have to take any cut at all."

"Now, wait a minute," said Jackie angrily.

"Hold on, hold on, girls," said Rick, grinning at them. "Sandy, you've got a point there. I'm willing to go along with it. I get twenty bucks, and you girls each get twenty-six bucks, and Jackie doesn't take anything this time because there's no need for it." He grinned at Jackie. "Right, honey-girl?"

Jackie hesitated, but she knew there was no use fighting it. Rick and the others would have their own way. "I guess that's fair," she said, trying to act as though she didn't really mind. But inside she was thinking: *I'm going to unload you, Rick. I'm going to drop you, and I'm going to drop you hard.*

5

SATURDAY SHONE bright and clear. They left the house on Maple Street at ten that morning, in a two-car caravan. Jackie and Rick rode in the red MG, and behind them came a halfback named Ted Martin, driving a black Borgward station wagon, containing the other four girls.

It was three hundred miles to Anderson, and they did it in just under eight hours, including a stop for lunch. It was quarter to six when they arrived at the motel just outside of town.

The Anderson Motel was closed for the winter, had been closed for three months, while the owners were away in Florida operating their wintertime motel in that state. But one of the football players knew the owner, wrote to him, and got the keys and a written okay for the use of the place over the weekend. This player had taken the precaution of going to the nearest State Police barracks and showing the letter, so no state policemen would happen to drop by at the height of the party to find out how come all these people were in this supposedly closed motel.

Like most motels, this one was crescent-shaped, the middle third two stories high, with an apartment on the second floor for the owner and his family, and the thirds to either side one story high. There were sixteen units to the motel, an office in the middle, beneath the apartment, and a roofed sidewalk along the front of the motel, the roof having protected the sidewalk from most of the two snowfalls that had come this year.

The main party would be held upstairs, with occasional forays, a couple at a time, to one of the units down below. The five girls selected the units which would be their base of operations, unpacked their overnight bags, washed their faces, and rode into town to get something to eat. Rick went to the stadium and got the free tickets for the girls, and then he and Ted Martin, the halfback, had to report in, while the girls had dinner.

The tickets were good, considering that they were free, giving them seats on the Anderson thirty-yard line. They sat alone, just the five girls, their ten escorts all being involved in the game going on out there on the field. And Anderson was so far from Clifton that not very many of the Clifton undergraduates had come along to see the game.

The other side of the stadium was packed with home-team rooters, colorful in red scarves and bright sweaters, fronted by their leaping short-skirted cheerleaders. Since it was a night game, the stadium was ringed with lights which occasionally flashed a brilliant semaphore of sparkle from an uplifted flask across the way.

The girls hadn't brought flasks, and they soon wished they had. It was a cold night, windless but icy, and breath steamed from people in the stands, bundled in their sweaters and greatcoats, the girls wearing bunt scarves, the boys huddled in bulky coats and armed with blue earmuffs.

But it was an exciting game, particularly for the contingent from Clifton, and the girls soon forgot the cold. With their bulky padding and huge white helmets, none of the players could be recognized, and they had to go by the numbers on the backs of the jerseys, comparing them excitedly with the program to see just who had made that particular run or tackle.

Rick was a lineman, not readily noticeable among the twenty-one other players on the field. He was usually somewhere near the bottom of the pile-up, though he did make one spectacular play.

It was near the end of the third quarter. Clifton was leading at that time, 15 to 11, and Anderson was in possession of the ball. Anderson had been in possession of the ball almost all the way through the third quarter, this time marching from their own twenty-three yard line to the Clifton thirty. It was third down and seven yards to go for a first down. The Clifton quarterback, apparently expecting a third-down pass play, had set up a five-three-two-two defense, with Rick on the right side in the second row of linebackers.

At the hike, the Anderson line broke wide, the Anderson backfield crisscrossed the receding quarterback in bewildering fashion, and the quarterback raced straight back as though fully intending to pass.

Jackie, by now, was used to recognizing the players by their numbers. Rick was thirty-seven, the number blazoned white and big across the back of his purple jersey. She saw him run a step toward the line when the ball was hiked, then stop and pivot and dash toward the sidelines.

Rick was the first one to see that the quarterback no longer had the ball. He'd handed off to the right halfback, who had streaked wide behind his line and was making a wide curve around his left end, almost to the sidelines.

He was out too far for Rick to catch up with him at the line of scrimmage. The halfback barreled across, nowhere near anyone on the Clifton team, and a groan went up from a sparsely seated Clifton side of the stadium. One Anderson halfback was running all alone with the ball. Twenty other players were completely out of it, back there in the middle of the field around the line of scrimmage, picking themselves up and looking around to see what had happened.

That left Rick, running his heart out. The Clifton partisans on this side of the stadium were on their feet screaming, "Stop him! Stop him!" And the much larger Anderson fans across the way were also standing, roaring out, "Go! Make a touchdown! Go!"

And Rick brought him down on the eight-yard line.

There was bedlam in the stands, at least on the Clifton side. For that moment, Jackie completely forgot her irritation with Rick. He had saved the day, he was big, white number 37 out there on the field, who had run his heart out and brought his man down on the eight.

It wasn't a touchdown, but it was a first down. Anderson tried for four downs to reach the goal line, all four on the ground, hitting the middle of the line, then the left side, then the middle twice more.

And they lost the ball on downs, on the two-yard line. Clifton passed and ran the ball up to the thirty, the third quarter became the fourth quarter, Clifton kicked the ball away on a fourth down and six, and Anderson raced the clock.

Across the way, the stands were going wild. The Anderson band, in blue and gold uniforms, played loudly and raucously and not quite in tune. The girl cheerleaders leaped and cavorted, shouting through blue megaphones. The Anderson mascot, a billy goat, pawed the turf in nervousness. The lights reflected from tilted flasks. The sound of desperate cheers roared out from the Anderson stands.

Anderson marched, and faltered, and lost the ball on downs. Clifton took long huddles, the quarterback gave long calls on the hike, and they didn't go for a single pass play, but ran every play on the ground. Clifton already had a winning score. All they had to do was wait out the clock.

The fourth quarter, as a result, was slow and uneven. Most of the time, Clifton had the ball and was sitting on it. Every once in a while—three times in the whole quarter— Anderson got hold of the ball and tried desperately to score. But they tried too hard and their play execution was sloppy. And when, the third time they had possession of the ball, a long end-zone pass was intercepted by Jim Carmichael, a halfback who had been an occasional customer the house on Maple Street, and Carmichael ran it all the way out to the thirty-five before being drowned in a deluge of furious Anderson tacklers, it was all over but the final gun.

The final score, when that gun at last did sound, was Clifton 15, Anderson 11. And by an odd coincidence that was also the time. Eleven-fifteen.

There weren't many of the Clifton supporters present, but they were noisy. They boiled out onto the field the second the game was over, pummeling the backs of the weary, dirty-faced, grinning players, and rushing over to tear the Anderson goal posts down. Anderson students raced out to protect the goal posts, and the whole scene dissolved into chaos. The last thing Jackie saw before leaving the stands was the beginning of half a dozen fights and the arrival of a bunch of stadium policemen.

The hot-dog and soft-drink vendors along the ramps and beneath the stands were shouting for last-minute business, and getting it from a large number of hungry and/or thirsty spectators, so that the ramps were crowded. It took forever for Jackie and the other girls to get outside and around to the parking lot. They waited by the cars while the players showered and changed, and then they all drove out to the motel. The party began.

The party, at the outset, threatened to fall flat on its face, due to a sudden attack of shyness on the part of the young men who had arranged it all. Except for Rick and Jim Carmichael, none of the players had ever been customers of the Maple Street Five. They had all stuck rigidly to their training programs. These eight knew all five girls, but they knew them as classmates and fellow students, not as paid bed-partners, and they were having trouble adapting to the new conditions.

The party, at first, therefore, was nothing but awkward conversation, mainly about the game that had just been completed. Rick was congratulated time and again for his game-saving tackle, Jim Carmichael was congratulated again and again for his game-saving pass interception, and Phil

Crawford was congratulated again and again for the field goal he'd kicked which, though it hadn't been needed to win the game, after all, had nevertheless been a perfectly lovely field goal.

Each of the girls handled this sticky situation in her own way. Honey flung herself from boy to boy, loudly, waiting for something to happen. Laura picked the football player with the highest forehead, and started talking to him about politics. Jackie began making and distributing drinks—vodka and ginger ale, mainly, plus beer for two of the players—at a furious clip, talking all the while. Rita sat silently in a corner and drank. And Sandy gravitated to Rick and stayed there.

One of the players had brought along a radio. This was plugged in—the player who had arranged for this spot had also seen to it that the electricity was turned on for the weekend, which gave heat as well as light since there were electric heating units in each room—and after some fiddling around they found a station broadcasting music to which it was possible, at least theoretically, to dance while holding a girl.

Sandy started to dance with Rick, Jackie grabbed a football player at random and danced with him, and Laura danced with her political debate partner. Honey danced all by herself for a while, until a player, emboldened by vodka and the sway of Honey's hips, stepped into her arms and she clung delightedly to him.

Someone else asked Rita to dance, and she did, but Jackie, watching Rita out of the corner of her eye, saw that the girl was having a hard time acting as though she were enjoying herself. *I hope to God she doesn't goof up,* Jackie thought desperately, and wondered if Laura had thought to bring any of her tranquilizers along. It might be a good idea, she thought, to keep Rita primed with tranquilizers on a permanent basis.

The party gradually came to life, though no one yet had taken advantage of the units downstairs. All the boys seemed to be waiting for somebody else to start the parade. They danced, the football players talked about football, the girls listened, and Jackie kept the glasses filled and an eye on Rita, who was drinking too much too fast. Unfortunately the drinks weren't having much of a tranquilizing effect.

Jackie was paired with Ted Martin for a while. The halfback was a big awkward-looking crew-cut senior, with a healthy smile and a surprisingly soft voice. He talked, inevitably, about football, and Jackie listened politely, showing as much enthusiasm as possible, while keeping a worried eye on Rita, across the room with two boys. The boys were doing all the talking, she noticed, and Rita wasn't doing too good a job acting as though she were listening.

The party had been going for an hour, and still was as decorous as though there were chaperones in every corner, when Jackie saw Rita getting ready to cry. It wouldn't be noticeable to the boys yet, but Jackie knew Rita better, and knew that tears were on their way, and it would only be a matter of minutes.

She excused herself as quickly as possible from Ted Martin, crossed the room, and put a hand on the shoulder of each of the boys with Rita. "Excuse me, gents," she said, "but I've got to talk girl-talk with Rita for a couple of minutes. Is it okay?"

They looked relieved, which was a bad sign, and one of them said, "Sure thing."

"You wait right here," Jackie told them, "and we'll be back in just a couple of minutes. Come on, Rita, let's go for a little walk."

"All right," said Rita. Her voice was slurred, and her eyes dull. *My God,* thought Jackie, *she's drunk already. And she's going to get maudlin in a minute. If only she'll wait at least until we're out of the room, that's all I ask.*

They left the living room together, walking through the owner's apartment to a bedroom at the far end. They were both silent until they reached the room and Jackie had shut the door. Rita sat down on the edge of the bed and said, "I'm sorry, Jackie. I don't know—it's just too much, it's—it's different from at home. I don't feel right doing—I'm sorry, Jackie, I'm really sorry."

Jackie sat down beside her and put an arm around her shoulder. "I know, Rita," she said. "I know how you feel. But this is important tonight. It really is."

"I know it is, Jackie. I'm sorry, I really am. I've been try-ing to act right, but I'm just so miserable, I—" And then the tears finally did come, and she huddled against Jackie, trem-bling, her body shivering as she sobbed.

Jackie held her, the one arm strong and secure around the other girl's shoulders, the other hand gently smoothing Rita's hair. "It's okay, honey," she whispered, her face pressed to Rita's hair. "It's okay, you just cry it out. Get it out of your system. It'll be all right."

"I'm so sorry, Jackie, so sorry," Rita gasped, still crying, and clung closer.

If I were a man, Jackie thought. *If I were only a man, Rita.*

At that moment, Rita raised her face, pale and frightened and tear-stained, and without planning it, without thinking,

Jackie bent her own head down and kissed the other girl on the lips, her arms tightening around Rita's body.

And Rita responded. Her own arms came up to encircle Jackie, her lips parted for Jackie's questing tongue, her body was pressed close to Jackie. Slowly they lay back together on the bed, and Jackie's lips moved from Rita's lips, across her satin-smooth cheek to the line of her throat and to her ear.

"Oh, yes," whispered Rita, "Oh, yes, Jackie, yes. Oh, I've wished you would do this. I've wanted you to do this so badly. I've only stayed there because of you, only because of you. I couldn't have stood it if it hadn't been for you. I've wanted you to do this for so long. Here, let me help. Oh, darling, anything for you. It's been so long. I'd lie awake at night and wish for you."

"I never knew," whispered Jackie, and then they were both silent, lost in the swoon and violent wonder of passion and ecstasy, their bodies intimately joined, their soft mouths and eager hands taking their will of each other.

Before they went back to the party, once they were dressed again, Rita said, "I'll be all right now. I really will. I'll smile and make them happy and do everything right. You'll see."

"I know you will, honey," said Jackie. She kissed the other girl lightly on the cheek and whispered, "We'd better go back now."

They walked back through the apartment to the living room, and found the party had grown livelier while they were gone. Only two of the girls were present now, Laura and Sandy, Honey having apparently managed to get some-body to go downstairs with her. But there were still ten men present, which meant someone else must have arrived in the meantime.

Someone else had. Professor Dan Blake, of Modes of Writing 201!

Jackie spied him, standing by the front door, and she almost fainted. The whole thing had blown up in their faces. Blake had caught them somehow. He must have heard somebody talking. *Now Dean Kelland will know,* she thought, *and everybody else, and it's all over with now. I'll be thrown out for sure, and maybe sent to jail.*

But then she realized that the party was still going on. None of the people in the room seemed the least upset by Professor Blake's presence. When she looked she saw that Professor Blake was holding a glass in his hand and was looking sheepish and embarrassed.

"Hey, Jackie!" somebody shouted. "Come on over here!" It was Ed Archer, a lineman on the football team, one of the veterans going to school on the GI Bill. He was standing next to Professor Blake, beaming from ear to ear, and motioning madly for Jackie to come over.

"I'll go be a party girl," whispered Rita, and she moved away into the crowd, a bright smile already on her face.

"Yes," whispered Jackie, though Rita was already out of hearing range. But seeing Blake there so suddenly had thrown her off balance. That, and what had just happened with Rita in the bedroom. She was having trouble adapting to all of this.

She weaved her way through the people, across the room to Blake and Ed Archer, smiling, trying to look poised and in complete control of herself, and as soon as she reached them Archer said, "Dan Blake, I want you to meet the best little girl on campus, Jackie Hayes. Jackie, the most miserably married man in history, Dan."

Blake's smile, too, was sheepish as he said, "Miss Hayes and I have met. But under somewhat different circumstances."

"I'm in Modes of Writing 201," Jackie explained to Archer. "Professor Blake's class."

"Oh," said Archer happily. "Then you're old friends. Jackie, I'll tell you how it is." He was half-lit and very, very happy. "I don't know if you've ever met Dan's wife—"

"I haven't," Jackie admitted.

"Well," said Archer, "I don't think Dan would mind if I told you that she is probably the worst woman to come along since they closed the Garden of Eden." He looked to Blake for confirmation. "Isn't that right, Dan?"

Blake was still being sheepish. "Ethel isn't the gentlest woman in the world," he said.

"Talk about understatement!" exclaimed Archer. "Jackie, honey, Dan here is a drinking buddy of mine. He can't very well hang around home every night, with old Ethel shrilling away at him. And besides, there's nothing else to hang around home for, Ethel being a good place to store frozen foods, if you get my meaning."

Embarrassed, Blake downed his drink. His sheepishness was slowly changing to anger.

"So Dan and I," continued Archer loudly, "we might get together four, five nights a week at Whitey's—you know the place? I mean, that's where I hang out to do my drinking, and that's where Dan hangs out to do *his* drinking, so with one thing and another we've gotten to be good drinking buddies. Ain't that right, Dan?"

"That's right," said Blake shortly.

"So anyway," Archer roared on, oblivious to the effect he was having on Blake, "I knew Dan was coming down to watch the old ball game—didn't we tromp them, though?—and I said to myself, I said, 'Ed, old Dan Blake needs a good time. Old Dan Blake needs a hot lay, and that's the truth. And here's this goddamn party we've got set up, and why don't I just go find Dan Blake after the game and bring him on to the party?' You know what I mean?"

"I know what you mean," agreed Jackie, and she was beginning to feel very sorry for Dan Blake, not only because of his wife and his problems at home, but also for the position he now found himself in, having to stand here and be polite while loud-mouthed Archer tromped all over his self-respect.

And Archer wasn't finished yet. "If you want a few extra bucks, Jackie," he boomed, "on account of—"

"It's all right," said Jackie quickly, wanting to spare Blake at least this little bit of humiliation. "Professor Blake is our guest."

Blake, surprisingly, bowed from the waist, and his smile this time was frank and natural. "Thank you, Miss Hayes," he said.

He's being gallant, Jackie thought. *He's weathering the storm beautifully.* She smiled back and said, "I think you ought to call me Jackie."

"Not until you call me Dan," he said.

"Fine." She held out her hand and smiled at him. "How are you, Dan?"

"Fine," he said, taking her hand, "And how are you, Jackie?"

"Just wonderful," she said.

"I'm Ed," said Archer loudly, "and I'm thirsty." And he veered away.

"So am I," admitted Blake.

"Come on," Jackie said, still holding his hand. "I'll show you where the makings are."

Their drinks made, they sat down together on a sofa, and Jackie took a second to check the house. Honey was back, but Sandy and Laura were both gone, and Rita was being animated in the middle of a group of boys. *Good girl,* Jackie thought, *you come through when it's needed, don't you?* As she watched, Honey headed for the door and the stairs again, and this time three boys went with her and Honey looked very bright-eyed and anticipatory. Jackie tried to visualize what *that* was going to look like, and couldn't do it. *It's impossible,* she thought, and shook her head.

Blake said, "What is it?"

Another doodle, Jackie thought. "Nothing," she said aloud. "I was just thinking, that's all."

"I'm not sure why I came here," Blake said suddenly. "It wasn't really for the reason Ed Archer suggested so loudly."

"I know," said Jackie, feeling that Blake was telling the truth.

"I was pretty sure I shouldn't come at all," Blake went on. "A member of the faculty at a party like this—I thought I would probably destroy the mood." He smiled again, the smile somewhat more firmly in place than any of the ones that had preceded it. "I notice I was wrong," he said.

"A lot of bottles were emptied before you got here," Jackie explained.

"I imagine that's part of it. Anyway, I knew I shouldn't come. Aside from ruining the party, there was the problem of my own reputation. If it ever got out that I had come to a party like this—"

Jackie laughed, interrupting him. "We'd be in worse shape than you," she told him.

"You're probably right. At any rate, the point is, all my reasoning to the contrary, I did have to come here tonight, for one reason and one reason only."

"Curiosity," suggested Jackie.

"Exactly," agreed Blake. "We faculty people labor under the fond delusion that we know what's going on in the world, or at least what's going on on-campus. To suddenly discover a thriving whorehouse—if you'll pardon the word—"

"I'll pardon it," smiled Jackie.

"Thank you. A thriving whorehouse just outside the campus gate—actually, a few blocks away, but you get my meaning—and staffed totally by co-eds and deriving its cus- tomers entirely from the male population of the student body—to suddenly find out that this thing has been going on for months under my very nose—and Dean Kelland's nose, and everybody else's nose—well, you'll have to admit it's a little fantastic."

"I suppose it is," admitted Jackie.

"I had heard rumors of something similar to this in one of the state universities in the Midwest," he said, "a number of years ago, and I suppose it is one of those things that happens every once in a while, but to discover it an already prosperous business in one's own college is astonishing. And curiosity is the mildest word to use for what impelled me here tonight."

Jackie quickly checked the house again. Rita was gone now, and Sandy and Honey were still away, but Laura was back. Two boys were sleeping on the floor in a corner. Honey was still gone. A series of improbable pictures flashed through Jackie's mind, and then she realized Blake was talking again, and she returned her attention to him.

He was saying, "You're the brains behind all this, I understand. The one who started it all in the first place, I mean."

"I guess so," she said. She wished he would find another topic of conversation. Suddenly, she was bored with discussion on how astounding and fantastic it was for her to put herself through college this way once her parents were no longer in any position to support her.

He seemed to sense her mood, for he said, "I should stop talking about it, is that right?"

"It's a party," she said. "You can talk about whatever you want."

"No," he said. "There's no need to be extra polite to me. I'm a party crasher, no more and no less. I'll sit quietly here and try not to get in anyone's way. You go on and mingle with your guests."

"No, that's all right."

"It isn't, and I know it isn't. I'd rather not leave yet, but I will if you won't simply ignore me for a while."

She looked at him, saw he was serious, and smiled. "All right," she said. "But I'll come back later on, and we can talk some more."

"Fine," he said. "In the meantime, I'll deplete the liquor supply."

After she had made two trips downstairs, Jackie suddenly remembered Blake again. She glanced over at the sofa. He was still sitting there, but he was now hunched forward, elbows on knees and hands hanging down between his knees, both hands encircling an empty glass.

He looked more morose and sorrowful than anyone she had ever seen, almost like an unloved Saint Bernard dog, and she decided suddenly that it was her job to cheer him up and make him a much more active member of the party. She excused herself from the group she was with, and went over to sit down beside Blake again.

"You look properly miserable," she said.

He looked up, the sheepish smile coming back to his face. "I was trying to think up enough energy to get off this sofa and go home," he said. "My reasoning was right, after all. I shouldn't have come here."

"Nonsense," she said briskly. "From the look of you, this party was what you needed more than anything else in the world. It's just that you won't get into the swing of things." She hooked an arm through his and smiled at him. "It's really quite easy to relax," she told him, "once you set your mind to it."

"Do you think so?"

It was at that moment that Honey made her grand entrance. She burst into the room and shouted, "It is *freezing* outside!" And it was no wonder she thought so, since she had had to walk from her unit along the outside sidewalk to the downstairs entrance of the apartment, and she had done it in the nude.

Her shout had attracted everybody's attention, and her nudity had seen to it that she *kept* everybody's attention. She had a beautiful body, warm and pliant, her breasts full and firm, the nipples taut and erect from the cold, and she looked absolutely delighted with life in all its many aspects. The three boys she had gone downstairs with so long ago trooped in now, looking weary, and scattered through the room.

In the sudden silence that had followed Honey's entrance, two-beat jazz with a snarling trumpet solo filled the room from the radio, and Honey flung her arms over her head, shouted, "Hotcha!" and started to dance.

That's all we needed, thought Jackie. *Honey, dancing in the nude.*

Two or three boys started clapping in time to the music, and most of the rest of them took it up, and Honey whirled around the room, graceful and excited, her magnificent body, after a moment, gleaming with perspiration.

Jackie glanced at Blake, and saw him watching Honey with eyes that had suddenly become bright and hard. *I'll let you watch awhile,* she thought to herself, *and then I am going to take you downstairs, Professor Dan Blake, and when you come back upstairs you are going to be the life of the party.*

One boy reached out and smacked Honey on the rump as she danced by, and she shouted again. Her dancing was growing progressively more complicated and more suggestive as she writhed her hips and shoulders and rotated her loins in an exaggerated version of the "grind." Her face was now flushed and sweating, her mouth wide open, her head snapping back and forth in time to the music and the clapping and the movement of her feet on the floor.

A circle had been cleared, almost magically, in the middle of the floor, where Honey was dancing. Suddenly Ed Archer stepped into the middle of that circle, and he was very drunk and just as nude as Honey. He stood there and shouted, "Hotcha yourself, baby!" and whooped with laughter.

Honey saw him and danced straight at him. When she bowled into him they toppled together to the floor in a scramble of naked arms and legs, and the circle closed in just slightly while the others cheered and clapped. Then Honey rose from the tangle, laughing wildly and whirled away. One of the football players rushed toward her, pulling her to the stairs while Archer had rolled—or had *been* rolled—over against a wall, where he began to snore peacefully.

Jackie leaned close to Blake, so that when she whispered to him her breath would tickle his ear, and she murmured, "Come with me."

He got to his feet wordlessly. She took his hand as they crossed the room and went through the doorway and down the stairs and outside to the moonlit snow-covered cold. They turned left, into the first unit they came to, which Jackie had claimed for herself. When she put her hand out to turn the light on he said, "No," and reached for her.

They were silent until they came to the bed, and then she reached up and touched his chest and said, "Dan, if we do it in the dark you won't be doing it with me, it won't be really happening."

He was silent for so long that she thought he just wasn't going to answer, and then he moved back from her and away, and she heard him crossing the room. The switch clicked, and the room flared with light. She blinked, and by the time she was able to see, he was standing over her, staring down at her.

She whispered, "Am I all right, Dan?"

"You're beautiful," he whispered back. "You're the most beautiful thing I've ever seen."

"Lie down with me, Dan," she murmured.

He stretched out beside her on the bed. "You *are* a woman," he whispered, as though telling himself more than her. "You're not a little girl, not just a student, you're a woman. I've needed a woman, Jackie. I don't know how long I've needed a woman."

She was silent, not knowing how to answer that, understanding the delicacy of this moment.

"You know I'm married," he said softly. "But that doesn't mean anything. I can be married, and still need a woman."

He moved suddenly, burying his face between her breasts, clinging to her with hurting hands. "I talk too much," he cried, his voice muffled by her flesh. "I've always talked too much."

"Hush, Dan," she murmured. "You don't talk too much. Hush, dear. Come on."

He raised himself slowly, and came to her, kissing her at first gently and then with increasing passion. She returned his kisses, yielding her breasts and shoulders and throat to the soft, almost timid stroking of his hands. She guided his lips to the warm trembling peaks of her breasts, feeling a great tremor of sensation roll through him. Then he clasped her body savagely to him and they were joined in an eager giving and taking, arms and legs entwined, the room around them and the night outside dissolving in a blur of mindless ecstasy.

They were sitting up together in the bed, side by side, smoking, and he was talking in a dull monotone about his wife. She was only barely listening to him, most of her attention was on herself and on what they had just done together, for Dan Blake was so completely different from the bandy roosters she was used to, so much stronger, so much more a man, that it was almost as though this had been the first time again, and she was astonished at the reaction in her, at the softness within her hard shell that made her want to cling to this man. When they had come down here, she had been the strong one, he the weak, she had been soothing and protecting him. And now the needs were reversed. She felt suddenly young and weak. She wanted no more than Dan Blake's arms around her, and she didn't even want to think about going upstairs.

He was talking in a monotone about his wife, and with a small part of her attention she was getting the gist of his story. He had met his wife in college, when she had been— or at least had seemed to be—a young, gentle and altogether lovable girl. They had been married now for ten years, and each year it had grown worse.

They had never been sexually compatible—not from the very beginning. He had discovered that on their honeymoon. Yes, he had waited—she had wanted to wait. And it didn't take long for him to realize that she was physically cold, that she got no pleasure at all from their lovemaking. He had tried to get her to go to a doctor, but she wouldn't, she never had.

And it had grown worse. From indifference, her attitude had changed to active distaste. And then she had found her real passion in life, and that had been faculty politics, and his young and gentle Ethel had quite rapidly become an accomplished nag. He didn't try to get published in the journals— an absolute necessity for a professor who would get ahead in the scholastic world—and she nagged at him for that. He didn't fight hard enough for tenure at Clifton, and she nagged at him for that. He devoted too much of his time and attention to his classes and his students, and too little time and attention to research and outside projects which could help him build a name and a reputation, and she nagged at him for that.

He continued to talk, looking blankly across the room at the door, and gradually she began to listen more closely to what he was saying. And when she did, the spell was broken.

It had only been sex, after all. That she could have been fooled this way, that she could have built up symbolisms of strength and weakness from what was only sexual maturity and sexual skill—that could mean only that she was tired and that she had drunk too much. Dan Blake was the weakling she had thought him upstairs, and now both her sympathy and that other weaker emotion were gone, and she felt only boredom. He deserved the wife he had, she thought, he would never be able to hold any other kind.

She stubbed her cigarette out in the ash tray on the bed-side table and got to her feet. "We'd better go back upstairs," she said, interrupting the monotonous flow of his reminis-cences.

He looked up, as though surprised to realize that she was still there. "Yes," he said. He got up from the bed, reaching for his clothes, and then paused and looked at her. "Again," he said. "When? I want to see you again."

"It's my business, you know," she reminded him. "This was just something special tonight."

"I know that," he said. "I'd pay you, of course. I would-n't ask for—for anything. But when?"

She considered, and she was too bored with him to want to try to be diplomatic with him. "See me after class on Monday," she said. "I'll make an appointment for you."

His face froze. "I see," he said dully, and he proceeded doggedly to put on his clothes.

6

JACKIE DIDN'T GO HOME for Christmas vacation. She knew what home would be like, and she wanted no part of it.

In the first place, her father would be constantly underfoot, since there was no mention in any of her mother's letters that he had found a new job or even that he was making any attempt to find one.

In the second place, her mother, with that horribly boomeranging desire to smooth over everything in sight and keep all the ugly spots hidden—which was her major characteristic—would be prattling and simpering twenty-four hours a day, trying to drown out the miserable facts of life in a flood of chatter, and it was almost inevitable that one of the topics of conversation she would leap on with both feet would be Jackie's wonderful secretarial job in Springfield, and Jackie just didn't feel up to inventing a leakproof series of lies with which to answer her mother's questions.

And in the third place, she had the sneaky suspicion that her father would want her to sell the MG. There had been hints in that direction already in her mother's letters, hints which she had parried by stating forcefully that she needed the car to get to her job in Springfield. Since she was now sending twenty or twenty-five dollars home each week, as a result of that job, this was sufficient to keep the hints at least to a minimum.

When Christmas vacation time came along, she wrote one of her own rare letters home. Usually, she simply sent a money order and let it go at that. But now she wrote a letter, explaining that she wanted to stay in Clifton over vacation because her boss wanted her to work full-time during the two weeks when there was no school.

Her mother, in her answering letter back, agreed readily enough, and Jackie thought she could understand why. This way, Jackie would not be one more mouth to feed for two weeks, and Mama could avoid the strain of her presence in the house under such different and difficult circumstances.

The other girls all went home over vacation, as did Rick, and Jackie temporarily closed the Maple Street house, moving completely back into the old apartment, for which she was still paying rent. Her customers had all gone home for vacation, too, all but one of them. Dan Blake.

Blake was Jackie's customer, the only customer who came exclusively to one girl. From the outset of the group operation, Jackie had seen to it that she scheduled the regular customers to different girls all the time, switching them steadily around. She didn't want any grand passions developing in the Maple Street house, with the result that one or more of her girls would retire from activity.

Blake was the exception, and he was the exception for a purpose. He was the only non-student who came to the house. He was completely lost on Jackie, and Jackie, after that one moment of weakness the first time they had gone to bed together, had never for a moment doubted that she could handle him completely. The time was going to come, she knew, when Rick was going to be more of a hindrance than a help, and when that time finally did arrive, Blake might prove very useful.

Given his head, Blake would undoubtedly have spent his entire salary in the Maple Street house, but Jackie was too smart to give him his head. She limited him to no more than two appearances a week, and he never knew in advance what night he would be next allowed to visit.

Jackie did her best to keep his visits from developing any sort of pattern. She didn't want an every-Tuesday-and-Friday type of setup, which could too readily become routine in Blake's mind, lessening Jackie's impact on him.

On the Friday before vacation was to begin, the last day of classes, Blake stopped her just after the Modes of Writing class and said, "Are you going home over vacation, Jackie?"

She had been intending to say yes, so she could have the next two weeks fully to herself, but now she saw the advantage of having no break in the relationship between herself and Blake and so she said, "No, I'm not. You can come over to my old apartment"—she gave him the address—"on Monday night, if you want."

"What time?" he asked immediately.

"Ten o'clock." She held a warning finger up. "No earlier, Dan."

"Not a minute," he agreed. "Ten o'clock on the dot."

"Fine." She smiled at him and went on her way. And on Monday night she restricted him to one hour just as though they were at the Maple Street house and there was another customer waiting. "When?" he asked her. She shrugged, considering. "Friday," she said.

"No earlier?" he demanded. "Jackie, you don't have anything else to do now. Why not tomorrow night?"

"Friday," she said coldly. "Ten o'clock. Or not at all."

He came on Friday, at ten o'clock.

With the end of vacation, Jackie had Rita to contend with again. It was immediately obvious that the girl should never have gone home, but should have stayed in Clifton with Jackie. Her family, from what Jackie had gathered during occasional conversations with Rita, was of the very poor but very pious type.

This was Rita's background, and she had dropped right into the middle of it again, going there straight from Maple Street in Clifton, with the result that she was now literally squirming with guilt, and Jackie's first sight of the girl, after vacation, was of Rita coming out of the church across the street, head bowed and hands clasped, and walking across the street to the house with heavy tread and dragging feet, for all the world like a condemned prisoner on the way to the gallows.

Jackie met her at the door. "Come on in, honey," she said. "You look as though you could use a drink."

Rita tried to smile, but it didn't work. Her face was pale, and getting thinner, and her hands were in nervous motion together in front of her. "Jackie," she said, pleadingly, as though asking Jackie to do something to smooth everything out for her, make everything all right and nothing painful.

"Come on in, baby," said Jackie. She took the other girl's arm and led her through the house to the kitchen. Rita sat heavily at the kitchen table while Jackie made them both drinks.

In the two weeks between the football players' party and the beginning of Christmas vacation, Jackie and Rita had gone to bed together three more times. Each time, Rita was thenceforth brighter and happier for the next few days, better able to convincingly play her part for the customers. And each time, Jackie got more nervous.

Because it was stupid—it was really and truly stupid. She wasn't a lesbian. And she still enjoyed going to bed with men. Therefore, there was no sense, no purpose, no *reason* behind this affair with Rita.

And particularly not with Rita. Of all the girls there, particularly not with Rita. Honey was certainly sexier and more passionate, Laura was far more intelligent, and Sandy was much closer to Jackie's own type. But Jackie felt no sexual desire for any of them at all, or for any other girl. Only for Rita.

During vacation, when she had been alone and had time to think things through clearly, she had come to a decision and had promised herself to act on it as soon as vacation was over. Her decision was to break with Rita. It was stupid to let it go on any longer, stupid to succumb to such a ridiculous craving. And the house would be far better without Rita in it. She wasn't really happy there, as the others were, it just wasn't the place for her. Jackie had made the decision, clearly and calmly and after much thought, and she had determined to act upon it, to get rid of Rita as soon as vacation was over.

And now, here was Rita in the kitchen of the Maple Street house. The time had come to act upon the decision, and Jackie found she couldn't do it. The same stupid idiotic desire was on her again, and she knew she couldn't do it. She couldn't send Rita away. It had been two weeks, and she wanted Rita more than ever.

"I was to church," said Rita dully. She sat heavy and limp at the kitchen table, one arm lying out straight on the table, the drink ignored in front of her. She looked at her hand on the table as she spoke. "I was to church, praying. I didn't want to come back here, Jackie. I prayed for strength not to come back here. Every day, at home, I'd look at my mother, and I'd think, *What if she knew? What if she ever found out? It would kill her.* And I promised myself I wouldn't come back here. I'd live in the dorm again and never even see you again."

Maybe she'll do it herself, Jackie was thinking. *I can't say it, I want to say it and I can't, to tell her to pack and go, to leave here and never come back. I can't say it, though I want it, and now maybe she'll say it for me.*

Rita stirred and shook her head. "I kept seeing you," she said, "in my mind's eye. I kept hearing your voice, when you'd say, 'Come down to my room tonight, after midnight.' I stayed in there as long as I could, because I didn't want to come back here at all."

Rita's monotonous voice stopped and still Jackie was silent. *I won't speak,* she thought, *and then maybe Rita will say it for herself. Maybe she'll go away if I don't say anything.*

But Rita looked up at last and said, "Do you want me to go away, Jackie?"

Jackie hung fire, her mouth open, two sets of words try-ing to claw their way out of her throat. Finally, she swept one arm aside in an angry gesture and turned away. "Come on," she said harshly, and fled to the bedroom.

The holidays were over, and the days ground into mo-tion again. There were five weeks before the February finals, and as final time approached the business slackened off somewhat, though every working hour there were at least two of the girls upstairs with customers. And Blake kept coming by, whenever Jackie allowed him to, looking more sheepish and guilty and impatient every time.

Meanwhile, Rick had suddenly switched his attention from Sandy back to Jackie.

It started a week after vacation. Jackie had only one cus-tomer that night, from ten till eleven, and afterward she was sitting in the kitchen in her bathrobe, reading a homework assignment and drinking coffee. Rick came in the back door, grinning, moving in that studied, affected way Jackie had come to know and detest. "Coffee hot?" he asked, and she motioned at the pot on the stove. He poured himself a cup and sat down beside her. He stretched, an exaggerated movement, and pointed at the book. "Blake's class?"

She nodded. She spoke to Rick as little as possible these days.

"What are you worried about?" he asked her. "There is-n't much chance he'll flunk you." And he laughed aloud.

"Keep it down," she snapped. "They're still working up-stairs."

"Making lots of money. Good girls. How come you aren't working, honey-girl?"

"This is my place," she said.

"Oh. You're the madam."

"That's right. And you're the pimp."

His expression didn't alter a bit, and he changed the subject—or seemed to—just as though he hadn't heard her. "You're seeing more and more of Blake lately, aren't you?"

"About the same as usual," she said.

"You mad at me for being with Sandy so much, honey-girl?"

"Don't give yourself credit, Ricky," she said.

"Don't call me Ricky. It makes me sound like a little kid."

She shrugged, looking at her open book.

"Listen," he said. He reached out suddenly and closed the book. "Listen to me, Jackie."

She turned a patient, blank face to him. "All right. What is it?"

"I was just trying to make you jealous, honey-girl," he said. The smile had left his face now, and he looked unusually serious. "Sandy doesn't mean anything to me."

"I couldn't care less," she said.

"Hey, look. Jackie, wait a second. Listen, you aren't still mad about that time I had to slap you around, are you?"

She turned back to the book and opened it. He shut it again and said. "Honey-girl, listen. That was months ago. What the heck do you want to hold a grudge that way for? You were being stubborn, and I was right, wasn't I? Didn't it work out I was right?"

"You're useful," she said, not looking at him.

"Jackie, come on. Let bygones be bygones. We used to get along fine together, remember?"

Something in his voice made her look at him, and the expression on his face—serious and worried—astonished her, and she suddenly gave him her complete attention.

He wants me again, she thought suddenly. *He wants me and he's asking for it. He isn't demanding. For Pete's sake he really wants me to like him again, he isn't trying to dominate me or anything.*

I can handle him, she realized all at once. *I didn't even know it, but I can handle him.*

Aloud, she said, "I remember, Rick. That was before you started acting like king of the mountain."

He shrugged it away. "You know how it was, Jackie," he said. "You didn't believe you needed me around. I had to act tougher than I felt. But I figured, you know, when you saw I'd been right all along—"

He let the sentence trail away, and she nodded, smiling. "Maybe I did get the wrong idea about you, Rick," she said. She got to her feet. "I think it would be fine if we were friends again."

He reached out and pulled her close, his arms around her waist, his cheek against her breast as he looked up at her. "We used to have good times, Jackie," he murmured. "Do you think maybe we could again?"

"Maybe," she said slowly. "Maybe it will all come back to me. We could find out."

"Come on, honey-girl," he said. He got to his feet, and led her to the bedroom.

She stood beside the bed, unmoving. He came around in front of her and kissed her, his arms gentle around her, and then he stripped away her clothing. She stood passive, neither helping him nor hindering him, and he undressed her as he might undress a mannequin. And when she was nude he stood in front of her, looking at her, smiling, and murmured, "I never should have gone away from you, honey-girl."

"You can always come back," she said softly, her lips curved in a slight half-smile.

He stood in front of her and stepped out of his own clothes, moving slowly and deliberately. She watched him—the slow grace, the almost dancelike quality, of his movements exciting her, and she had to fight to keep her body relaxed and her hands easy at her sides.

He came close to her again, enfolding her in his arms, and their flesh touched as he whispered, "We're the same type, honey-girl. We do well together."

"Rick," she whispered and shuddered, not understanding the strength of this excitement, frightened by it.

When he moved her to the bed, she went quickly, gratefully, and they came together with sudden violence.

They spent that night together. The next night he went back to Sandy, but the night after that he had returned to Jackie again, and after that he didn't go near Sandy at all.

And then it was impossible to be with Rita. She enjoyed going to bed with Rick, he was a lot of fun, but Rita was getting upset again, and Jackie didn't know what to do about it. Rita knew that Rick was spending his nights with Jackie once more, and Jackie caught her every once in a while glaring at Rick with unconcealed jealous hatred. And the same expression was beginning to come into her eyes when she looked at Blake.

It would be so simple without her, Jackie thought. *So simple.* The thought of being without her was so clear and good and simple, but there just wasn't any way to put the thought into practice.

It was a week before she had a chance to be alone with Rita, and then there finally came a night when Rita was free during the first hour, from nine till ten. Jackie knew that Rick never came to the house much before eleven, so she went upstairs at five after nine, when all the other girls had already closed their doors behind their first customers, and walked into Rita's room to find the girl returned to the habit of her first few weeks here, lying fully dressed on the bed with the lights off, staring at the ceiling.

When Jackie turned the lights on, Rita immediately sat up, blinking and white-faced, as though she had expected to see her mother standing there, or at least a squad of police. But when she recognized Jackie, she leaped up from the bed and ran into Jackie's arms.

Jackie pushed the door closed behind her, and held the quivering girl close for a minute. "Okay, Rita," she murmured. "It's all right, calm down, it's all right."

"I thought you gave me up," wept Rita. "I thought you were with *him* now." She didn't define whether she meant Rick or Blake, but Jackie assumed it was Rick who was worrying the girl.

"I have to be with him when he wants me," she said reassuringly. "I don't have any choice. But it doesn't mean anything, you know that." She edged the girl closer to the bed. "It's you I love," she murmured, "you know that, Rita. It's only you."

Half an hour later, coming down the stairs to the first floor again, Jackie had a lot to think about.

It was gone. Whatever it was that had drawn her to Rita, that had kept that stupid affair alive this long, was finished now. It had disappeared like smoke.

She hadn't known it, not until she had actually been in bed with Rita, and for the first time she could look at what they were doing together with a clinical and dispassionate eye and say honestly to herself—*I don't enjoy this. It means nothing to me.* Not until she could look at Rita's body, willing and pliant beside her in the bed, and know that she felt no rising of desire for that body, not until then had she realized that it was over.

Why? Why had it disappeared so rapidly, and so completely? The only thing that had changed had been Rick's return to her, and surely she wasn't in love with Rick. It wasn't as though the very nature of her business didn't give her enough male sexuality to keep her satisfied.

Whatever had done it, it was gone. Rita was now only pathetic, only a weakling like Blake, with the exception that Blake was useful—or might be, eventually—and that was something Rita could never be.

It's time to get rid of Rita, she thought. *I can do it now—if only I could have done it the day she came back from vacation, it would have been simpler then—but I can do it now. Gradually. I'll have to work it so that she thinks it's her own idea to leave, so she won't be mad at me and want to get even with me by talking to Dean Kelland.*

I hope, she thought, *that she doesn't get too repentant after this is all over, and figure the only way she can save her immortal soul is by shouting her confession from the rooftops.*

It would have to be done carefully, the unloading of Rita. But it could be done. There was no doubt of that now, it could be done.

Feeling better than she had in weeks, better and more purposeful, Jackie went out to the kitchen, started a pot of coffee, and sat down to wait for Rick.

But it was, after all, a good thing that she had kept Rita on for so long, and that she had decided to move slowly in getting rid of her. For it was from Rita that she learned about Rick and Sandy's sideline.

It was three days later, a Friday, at five in the afternoon. Jackie was at the desk in her bedroom, working on the account book. She had a complete fiscal record, the money each girl earned each week, the amounts paid out to Rick, the amounts the other girls paid to her, the amounts paid out in rent and gas and electric and the other expenses of keeping up the house, and on Friday afternoons she brought the book up to date. The rest of the week it was kept in a locked drawer in her desk.

She was making the entries in the Gross Earnings column when the knock came at the door. She always kept the door locked when she was working on the books this way.

She immediately called out, "Just a second," and put the record book back in its drawer and locked it. She then crossed the room and opened the door.

It was Rita, looking frightened, and Jackie immediately began to think of excuses for not going to bed with her.

But that wasn't what the girl was there for. "I have to talk to you, Jackie," she said, her voice a conspiratorial half-whisper. "It's kind of important."

"Come on in," Jackie said, and stood aside for the girl to enter.

Rita came in, and said, "We better close the door. We don't want anybody to hear."

"To hear what?"

"Close the door, Jackie. Please."

Rita's obvious agitation communicated itself to Jackie, and she obediently closed the door, then motioned for Rita to sit in the desk chair while she herself sat down on the edge of the bed. "What is it?" she asked.

"Bob told me about it," said Rita breathlessly. She and Bob Silver had been seeing each other again, weekends and afternoons, though Bob hadn't come back to the Maple Street house since that first time, nor had he ever been a customer of Rita's or anyone else's at the house.

"Told you about what?" Jackie prompted.

"Bob heard a couple of the other boys talking about it in the dormitory, and he came to ask me if it was true, because he said if it was true it was too dangerous and maybe I ought to leave here, after all." Rita said all that in one steady stream, and finally paused to inhale deeply.

"If what was true?" demanded Jackie. She hated long build-ups like this, and wished Rita would get to the point.

"The other boys said you could buy marijuana here," Rita said. "Pot, they called it. In little cigarettes. They said this was the only place in Clifton where you could buy it."

"Marijuana? You know better than that." Jackie was relieved at finding it was nothing at all, and she smiled and lit a cigarette. "I wouldn't have anything like that here," she said. "Bob's right, it would be too dangerous. We'd have the police on us in a flash if we ever tried anything like that. This way, the police never even notice us."

"The boys told Bob it wasn't you that was selling it," Rita said. "They said it was only Sandy. She was the only one who had it, and was selling it."

"Sandy?" Jackie was instantly alert again, and now wary. "What else did these boys have to say?" she asked.

"Well, Bob asked them where anybody would get marijuana from in a little town like Clifton. You know, how Sandy could get any to sell, because she practically never even leaves the house and she never goes anywhere out of town. Because Bob didn't believe them when they told him about the marijuana."

"Did they have any answer for him?"

"They said they'd heard—Sandy'd told somebody—that Rick went to Springfield for it, he knew somebody there who could get it from somewhere else, I don't know where. But that Rick was the one who brought it here, and then Sandy would sell it to boys when they were upstairs with her. They said she kept the marijuana cigarettes in a metal box, and the box was under her bed."

Jackie nodded grimly. "She always told me she kept her profits there. Maybe she used to."

"Do you think it's true?" Rita asked.

"I don't know," Jackie told her, though she knew well enough that it had to be true. "I'll find out, one way or another."

"I couldn't stay on here," said Rita. "You understand that, don't you? I'd be too scared to stay on here."

If only you would run away, Jackie thought savagely. Aloud, she said simply, "I'll find out about it, one way or another. Thanks for telling me, Rita."

"I wanted to know whether it was true or not."

"Thanks, Rita." Jackie propelled the other girl to and through the door, though it was obvious that Rita wanted to stay and talk about being scared. But Jackie had a lot to think about, and she could do her thinking better without Rita prattling at her elbow.

Alone in the room, she looked at herself in the mirror on the closet door, and muttered disgustedly, "You're a real brain, Jackie. *Honey-girl,* you're a whiz."

So Rick had come back to her. Of course he had. He had this sweet little racket running right under her nose, and he came back with her to be sure there wouldn't be any trouble if by any chance she did find out. He figured he'd have her under control by then, and if he stayed close enough to her she might never find out at all.

She wondered suddenly about Sandy, if Sandy was taking the stuff—smoking the stuff. It would be hard to tell, marijuana affected different people in different ways. And Sandy was always so silent and glum and uncommunicative anyway.

Now that she thought of it, she remembered reading somewhere that marijuana very often dulled sexual appetites, contrary to popular opinion and popular fiction. And that might be another reason why Rick had come back to her. With Sandy smoking marijuana—after working hours, Jackie hoped, at least she hoped Sandy would have sense enough to wait until after working hours—and then lying in the bed as stiff and uncaring as a log, Rick would naturally look for another girl to take Sandy's place. And if Sandy were affected that way, it wouldn't matter a bit to her that Rick was no longer spending his nights with her.

It had to stop. That's all there was to it. It had to stop, she had to figure out some way to be *sure* it was stopped.

She paced back and forth in the room for fifteen minutes, and finally made her decision. She left the room and went upstairs and into Sandy's room.

Sandy was in the bathroom, dressed only in panties, rinsing out stockings. She looked noncommittally at Jackie and said, "Hi."

"Hi," said Jackie. She didn't want Sandy to get the idea she knew, not ahead of time, so she did her best to be civil, and to smile naturally at the other girl.

"What's doing?" Sandy asked, without much interest.

"Little meeting tonight," Jackie told her. "After the last customer. You've got one at eleven tonight, haven't you?"

"Sure."

"Right after he leaves then. Couple minutes after midnight. Down in the kitchen."

"Okay," said Sandy. "I'll be there."

"Good," said Jackie.

Rick arrived at eleven-thirty. Jackie was sitting at the kitchen table when he came in. He made himself a pot of coffee, poured a cup for her, and sat down at her right. "How's the day?" he asked her.

"So-so."

"You tired?"

"Not very. I want to stay up for a while."

He looked at her. "Something wrong, honey-girl?"

She returned his gaze. "Not that I know of," she said levelly. "Why? Should there be something wrong?"

"Not by me," he said. "Feel like some gin rummy?"

"Not now."

There was silence for a minute, and then he said, "Did you hear? They're going to tear down the Student Union. Over the summer. They're going to build a new one."

She looked up, interested in spite of herself. "When will they start tearing the old one down?"

"May sometime. You'll have to find some place else for the appointments, huh?"

"I'll worry about that when the time comes," she said.

They were silent again for a while, and then Rick reached back to the shelf above the workboard and got a deck of cards. He played solitaire for a while, occasionally glancing out of the corner of his eye at Jackie, who sat stolid and silent to his left, and finally he put the cards down and said, "Something's eating you, honey-girl. What the hell's the matter with you?"

"I just don't feel like talking right now," she said.

He looked at her for a few seconds more, then shrugged and went back to the card game.

It was a long, silent half-hour before Sandy came walking in, looked at the two of them sitting there, and said, "I thought there was a meeting."

"Sit down," Jackie said. She nodded her head at the chair to her left, across from Rick.

Sandy looked guardedly at Rick, but Rick was giving his whole attention to the collecting and stacking of his cards, so she shrugged and walked around the table to sit where Jackie had motioned. "What is it?" she asked, looking from Rick to Jackie and back.

"I want to tell you two something," Jackie said quietly. "And I don't want you to interrupt until I'm finished."

"I knew there was something bugging you, honey-girl," said Rick pleasantly.

"If I ever hear," Jackie went on doggedly, "of another bit of marijuana being sold in this house, I'll close the house down. I'll drop out of school and I'll deliver Dean Kelland a letter naming names and places. I can go to some other school. I don't have to stand for this. This is my place, and we'll run it the way I want to run it, or we won't run it at all. Dope is going to draw police. I don't want it in this house."

There was silence after she was finished, and then Rick sighed and said, "I knew there was something bothering you, honey-girl, and I had a feeling this was it. Okay, Sandy, go on up and get it."

"Just a minute—" started Jackie.

"This'll just take a second, honey-girl," said Rick calmly. "Go on, Sandy, hurry it up."

Sandy left the kitchen. The other two waited silently until she came back, carrying an envelope which she handed to Rick. Rick set it on the table in front of Jackie.

Jackie looked at it, a thickly stuffed business-size envelope, and said, "What's this?"

"Take a look," Rick told her.

Jackie opened the envelope. Inside was a stack of five- and ten-dollar bills, and a sheet of typewriter paper. On the sheet of paper had been carefully written in ink a record of the purchase and sale of marijuana over a period of almost three months.

Jackie looked up at Rick again, puzzled. "What is all this?"

"Your cut," he said. "Your third. We've been setting a third of the profits aside for you every week, because we knew sooner or later you were going to have to be cut in. Sandy wanted to cut you in the very first day she moved in here, but I told her to wait. I told her you'd probably get on your high horse. I told her the best thing to do was wait awhile, until we could show you it was safe, until we could say, 'Look, we've been doing it all this while and there's never been any trouble.' Because, honey-girl, you're bullheaded, you know that, and you never will believe in advance that I'm right."

Jackie shook her head, and pushed the envelope away. "I don't want dope in this house," she said.

She was barefoot and now, under the table, Rick's shod foot was suddenly pressed lightly atop her right foot. He pressed down a bit and said softly, "Pick up your money, Jackie."

All at once, she remembered vividly the last time he had beaten her. She reached out and picked the envelope off the table.

"Good girl," he said. He produced a pen and set it down on the table in front of her. "Maybe you ought to sign a receipt," he said. "That account sheet will do. Just write, 'Received, my share, eighty-five dollars.' And sign your name."

She did so, knowing she had no choice, that he would beat her if necessary until she did sign it, and she was thinking: *Monday I've got to see Blake. The time has come. He got to help me get rid of Rick. Monday, I see Blake.*

And the part that hurt her worst was the sure knowledge that she was being cheated. Eighty-five dollars was nowhere near a third.

7

WHEN SHE HAD MADE HER THREAT about closing and exposing everyone concerned with it, Jackie had meant every word she had said. But now, of course, that was no longer possible. Rick and Sandy—Rick, really, since Sandy was obviously simply another girl that he was using, as he had all this time been using Jackie herself—now had a signed piece of paper from Jackie, acknowledging receipt of money gained from the sale of illegal narcotics in Jackie's own house. Rick had that piece of paper, and that meant that he also had Jackie's silence and Jackie's co-operation.

That's what he thought.

Because there was always Dan Blake. Jackie wasn't sure yet just how she could use Dan Blake, but she was sure of the simple fact that she was definitely going to use him.

Dan Blake was a faculty member, the closest thing to what passes for authority on a college campus. One way or another, he would be the rifle with which she would shoot Rick Marshall down.

The time had come. He had taken over her house, twenty per cent of her earnings—and she had no doubt but that he would throw her out of her own house and put Sandy in as madam in her place if Jackie proved to be too troublesome.

Throughout the long, quiet, inactive weekend, Jackie kept the one thought uppermost in her mind *I am going to talk to Blake.* She avoided Sandy, and she avoided Rick, and she waited.

Monday moved slowly, class plodding after class, and at last it was two o'clock, Modes of Writing was finished. Blake was at the head of the table putting his notes and books back in his scruffy briefcase, and the students were filing out of the room. Jackie stopped near Blake and said, quietly, "I want to see you tonight, Dan. Ten o'clock."

His face lit up. He didn't even question the reason for this sudden change. "I'll be there," he promised, and Jackie rewarded him with a smile, and went on her way, heading for the Student Union, where she would be stationed for the next hour, accepting appointments from her customers.

I'm going to get you, Rick, she thought. *I'm going to have Dan Blake, and I'm going to use him, and I'm going to get you.*

At quarter after nine that night, the doorbell rang at the Maple Street house. Jackie answered it, wondering which of her ten o'clock customers had come so early, and she almost fell over in a faint when she saw the two people standing outside on the porch.

There was C. Jerome Kelland, B.A., M.A., Ph.D., Dean of Clifton College.

And there was Agnes Lung Storm, B.A., M.A., Ph.D., Assistant to the Dean, Dean of Women, Clifton College.

Dean Kelland consulted a piece of paper in his hand. "Mister Maropolous, please," he said.

It took Jackie a couple of seconds to remember who Mister Maropolous was. And then she remembered that it was the landlord, the man who owned this building. And Honey was supposed to be his niece. That was how Sandy and Laura and Honey had permission to live off-campus, because Honey was Mister Maropolous' niece, and the other two girls were living here, too, with Honey.

Jackie, according to the school records, wasn't living at the Maple Street house. She and Rita were living with Jackie's "aunt" at the old apartment.

"Mister Maropolous," said Jackie quickly, "isn't here right now. But his niece is—Honey Bane. I'll call her. If you'd step into the living room?"

She led them into the living room, smiling cheerfully at them and praying that none of the nine o'clock customers decided to let out a shout from above right now, or chose this particular night to leave early.

Miss Storm, ancient and as round as a tugboat, inquired, "Do you live here, too?"

"No, I've come over to do some homework. I'll call Honey."

Jackie back-pedaled out of the living room, smiling and nodding, and raced upstairs. Honey and Laura and Sandy all had customers with them now. Jackie was terrified.

She rapped on Honey's door and burst in immediately. Ignoring the boy scrambling around on the bed, she whispered to Honey, "Dean Kelland's here! Him and Aggie Storm! They were asking for Maropolous!"

Honey sat up, nude and wide-eyed and divested of her boy. "What do they want?"

"I don't know. Get dressed, Honey, quick, and get downstairs. And remember you're Maropolous' niece. And you—" to the petrified boy, "—get under the bed. They may not come up here, but I'm not taking any chances. Under the bed."

Without pausing to see whether Honey or the boy were obeying, she dashed back out to the hall and paused to rip the name tags off the doors. Then she dashed into Laura's room, and Sandy's room after that, warning both girls to get dressed and both boys to get under the bed.

Rita was in the fourth room, fully dressed, and Jackie told her also what was going on, and said, "Remember, you don't live here. You live at the old apartment with me. We came over here to do homework. This is Mister Maropolous' room—he sleeps here. Hide all your stuff. Try to make the place look like a man's room. And get out of here as quick as you can and come downstairs."

She ran back and forth from room to room, inspecting, making sure things looked all right. Laura and Sandy were together in Laura's room, studying history in quiet tones, asking one another questions about the current assignment. Three boys were hiding under three beds. Everything looked fine.

Jackie went back out to the hall and started down the stairs, just as Dean Kelland and Dean of Women Storm and Honey Bane started up. "Frankly," the Dean was saying, "our records show that students who live on campus get consistently higher grades than those who live off-campus. There hasn't been an inspection of off-campus facilities for three years, and Dean Storm and myself decided to have what you might call a surprise inspection, to be sure our students off-campus were adequately housed."

"I'm real sorry uncle Georgio isn't here right now," Honey Bane said, and then the three of them came around the last turn and up to the hall. Jackie offered the Dean and the Dean of Women a sickly smile, and tried to become one with the wallpaper.

"I'm afraid my room's an awful mess," Honey said, laughing with embarrassment. "I never have been very good at cleaning up. Don't look under the bed, there's a ton of dust under there."

Dean Kelland was a firm and straight-backed, white-haired old man of military bearing and a nineteenth-century courtliness in his attitude toward women and children. He now smiled a military smile and said, "It isn't that kind of inspection at all, Miss Bane. We just want to be sure that the housing facilities are adequate, that there aren't too many distractions for study, and things of that type."

Honey opened the door to her room and stood aside. "There it is," she said, smiling hopefully at the two deans.

They didn't go into the room, for which Jackie could have kissed them. She looked past them, and from her angle of vision she could just barely see an elbow under the bed. She chewed painfully on her lower lip, trying by mental telepathy to tell the boy to move his elbow farther back out of sight.

But the deans didn't notice a thing. They looked in, smiling and nodding, and Dean Storm said, in her high-pitched, cracked, wheezing old lady's voice, "It seems like a pleasant room, doesn't it?"

"A desk for studying, I see," commented Dean Kelland. "Very good."

Dean Storm turned to Honey. "I believe there are two other girls living here with you," she said.

"Oh, sure," said Honey. "Laura and Sandy. They're around somewhere." She opened the door to Sandy's room and looked around inside. It was empty, or at least it *looked* empty. The deans stuck their noses into the room, but once again they didn't step inside or actually do any inspecting. They simply looked from the doorway, and Dean Kelland commented on the well-stocked bookcase and Dean Storm observed that the bed looked comfortable. Then Honey closed the door to that room and tried Laura's room.

Laura and Sandy were dressed, as was Honey. Jackie knew—but neither dean did—that the clothes they saw were all the clothes they wore. The sweaters and skirts covered nothing but girl. This was only noticeable in Honey's case; her sweater was curved a little too intricately in front for there to have been a bra beneath the sweater.

Dean Kelland, in his clipped and military manner combined with white-haired courtliness, explained all over again to Laura and Sandy about the inspection of off-campus student facilities and the disparity between the marks of students who lived on-campus and those who lived off-campus. "Although," he finished, "I don't believe any of you three living here are in any serious scholastic difficulty at the moment, are you?"

"No, sir," replied Laura, who was a straight-A student and always had been.

Dean Kelland turned to Jackie. "You're Jacqueline Hayes, aren't you?"

"That's right, sir," said Jackie.

The dean consulted his list again. "But you don't live here, do you? I have you down for another address, living with your aunt, isn't that right? You and another girl, a Rita Amherst."

"Yes, sir, that's right," said Jackie.

"Now you, young lady," said the dean, "are running into trouble. There's still time to catch up before the end of the semester, but at the moment you're in danger of failing at least two of your courses."

Jackie ducked her head, looking as shamefaced as possible. "Yes, sir, I know," she said. Jackie had always been more of a good-time girl than a good student. Now, devoting so much time and attention and energy to the house, her grades, always shaky, had started to fall below passing grade. She knew she had to make it up, or no matter how much money she had she still wouldn't be able to stay in school. She'd flunk out.

The only course she was sure she wouldn't flunk was Blake's course. And he was due here at ten o'clock tonight!

That thought hit her like a wet dishcloth in the face. It was only about twenty-five after nine, but what if Blake were to show up early? Or what if these two old biddies were to stick around for another half-hour, when Blake and all the ten o'clock customers would be showing up?

But Dean Kelland—bless his soul—was moving toward the stairs, saying to Jackie, "Is your aunt home now, do you think?"

"I don't know for sure," Jackie told him, thinking furiously. "She doesn't like to be home alone. She may be off to the movies right now."

"We'll stop over and check," he said, and led the way down the stairs, Dean of Women Agnes Lung Storm following him, Honey Bane next in line, and Jackie bringing up the rear.

At the foot of the stairs, Dean Kelland turned and spoke to Honey. "When your uncle comes home," he said, "I wish you'd tell him that we were here, and that we found this a most pleasant home, admirably planned for the privacy a student needs."

"I sure will," said Honey fervently.

Dean Kelland turned a jovially stern finger at Jackie. "And you, young lady," he said, with mock severity, "you'd better get cracking at the books."

"I will, sir," said Jackie, just as fervently. "I really will." And with that, the two deans left.

The boys, still shaking, were collected from under their respective beds. Honey suggested that, since it was only nine-thirty, they go right on now as though nothing had happened to interrupt them, but none of the boys seemed to be in the mood any more. Jackie got out her appointment book and rescheduled all three boys with the same three girls for other times later in the week, at no additional charge. "We'll call these rain checks," she said.

"You mean dean checks," said one of the boys, a husky six-footer who needed a shave, and who'd had a difficult time crawling under the bed. "And if it deans the next time I'm here, I'm through."

The boys dressed and left, the name tags were put back on the doors, and everything finally settled down. Jackie went out to the kitchen and looked at the clock. It was only twenty minutes to ten. It seemed impossible that only twenty-five minutes had gone by since Dean Kelland and Dean Storm had rung the doorbell.

They'd been a hectic twenty-five minutes.

Ten minutes later, it started again, but somewhat more seriously. The doorbell rang and Honey answered it this time, since she was, after all, the niece of the owner.

A woman was standing on the porch, looking grim and severe. "I want," she said sternly, "to speak to a Miss Jackie Hayes."

Honey was a bit confused at this, but Honey always knew what to do when confused. Be friendly. So she smiled sweetly and said, "Well, sure. Come on in."

The woman stepped into the house, glaring to left and right, and Honey closed the door, then said, "I'll call Jackie. I think she's in the kitchen. Would you like to sit down in the living room?"

"I'll wait here," said the woman coldly.

"Okay," said Honey, unoffended. She left the woman and walked through the house to the kitchen, where Jackie was sitting drinking coffee, dressed in skirt and sweater, slippers on her feet, recuperating from the visit of the deans. "Some woman to see you, Jackie," Honey said, offhandedly. "She acts mean."

Jackie got to her feet. She was expecting Blake in fifteen minutes. She hoped this wouldn't take long. "Who is it, do you know?"

Honey gave an exaggerated shrug and shook her head. "Beats me, Jackie. Never saw her before in my life."

"Hope it isn't somebody's mother," said Jackie fatalistically.

"Hardly," said Honey.

The two girls walked back to the front of the house. Honey went upstairs, to get ready for her ten o'clock customer, and Jackie strode over to the woman visitor, studying her carefully on the way.

She saw a woman of perhaps thirty, dressed in a severe tweed suit and 'sensible' shoes, her mouse-brown hair tied in a cruel bun at the back of her head, her hands clasped over a small black purse, lines of frowning discontent permanently imbedded in the skin around her eyes and mouth. Her nose was straight and sharp, her eyes cold and pale-blue, her lips a pale, thin line without cosmetics, her jawline too harsh to be feminine.

I don't know what this is, thought Jackie, *but from the looks of this old broad, it can't be anything but trouble.*

She stopped in front of the woman and attached a smile to her face. "Hello," she said, politely. "I'm Jackie Hayes."

"How do you do?" said the woman, with sardonic coldness. "I am Mrs. Daniel Blake. I believe you and I have some talking to do."

Jackie hoped the sudden plummeting of her heart into her stomach hadn't showed on her face. Rallying, she said, "Professor Blake's wife? How *do* you do? Won't you come into the living room?" But then she realized the time. The customers would be arriving in just a few minutes, and she amended that suggestion, saying, "Or perhaps the kitchen would be better. We could have a nice pot of coffee and sit around the kitchen table. I always think women can talk more readily over the kitchen table, don't you? At least, it works that way for me. A nice hot cup of coffee—"

She neither knew nor cared what she was saying, just so she managed to get this woman to the back of the house.

Out of the corner of her eye, she noticed Laura sitting in the living room, watching them carefully, and she supposed Laura had heard the woman introduce herself. She hoped Laura would have sense enough to warn everybody to stay out of the kitchen for a while.

Her mind was darting off in a million directions at once—the customers, Blake, Laura, Sandy, Rick, Honey, herself, Mrs. Blake—but she forced herself under control, telling herself firmly to think of only one thing at a time. If she thought of only one thing at a time she'd be all right, and the thing to think about right now was the shepherding of Mrs. Daniel Blake to the back of the house.

Mrs. Blake allowed herself to be led to the kitchen to a chair at the kitchen table, but when Jackie reached for the coffee pot, she said, "Miss Hayes, don't you think you've carried this domesticity far enough? We have things to talk about."

One thing at a time, thought Jackie frantically. *Wait it out. Let this woman take the lead. See where she wants to go.*

"All right," she said aloud. She sat down at the table opposite the woman and said, "If you want to talk, sure."

"I want to talk," said Mrs. Blake. "And I think you know what I want to talk about."

Jackie did her best to combine innocence, interest and guilelessness on her face all at once.

"I want to talk about my husband," continued Mrs. Blake inexorably. "My husband and you."

"Professor Blake?" asked Jackie innocently.

"I know, young lady," snapped Mrs. Blake. "Don't you think I know?"

"Know?" Jackie was growing more innocent by the second, and more wide-eyed.

"About you and my husband," said Mrs. Blake bitterly. "That you and my husband have been having a sordid affair for months. Don't you think I pay any attention at all to his comings and goings? Don't you think I've seen him come into this house?"

"Mrs. Blake, I—"

"Don't interrupt. I know it's you, and none of the other girls staying here." She leaned forward across the table. "Have you no shame?" she asked suddenly. "What do you suppose these other girls think of you, carrying on an affair with a married man?"

Jackie was so relieved all at once that she completely forgot to look innocent. *She doesn't know!* was all she could think. *She thinks it's just an affair. She doesn't know what's going on here at all!*

"There's no use denying anything," continued Mrs. Blake, completely unaware of the measure of relief she had just afforded Jackie. "There's no sense trying to hide it. I know it's you."

Jackie bowed her head, having now replaced the innocent expression by an expression of contriteness, almost of shame. She wasn't really thinking now. She couldn't think of anything except the fact that this woman didn't know the truth, after all. She was playing it by ear. "I won't try to deny anything," she said humbly.

The admission and the humility seemed to bolster Mrs. Blake's determination and righteousness. She sat back again, both hands flat on the table, and glared at Jackie. "It has to stop," she said. "You realize that. It has to stop. I won't put up with it any longer."

"Yes," whispered Jackie. Playing it by ear, almost unconsciously, she was doing a perfect job of portraying guilt and contrition and the overwhelming desire to make amends.

"You're young," said Mrs. Blake, softening somewhat at this complete collapse of her opponent. "I don't really hold you to blame. I have no doubt it was my husband who started all this."

"I'm as much to blame as he is," mumbled the humbled Jackie.

"Be that as it may," said Mrs. Blake. "This is what I demand. I want you to leave this school at once. Make whatever excuses to your parents and the school administration you like—I don't care. But I will not have you anywhere near my husband."

Time, Jackie was thinking. *I need time, time to think, time to plan, time to get this all straightened out. Think about one thing at a time, and play for time. Agree to anything—but not too readily, can't afford to make her suspicious.*

"Leave the school?" she echoed, timidly, her voice a study in bewilderment. "I can't do that. I couldn't do that, leave the school."

"It's that," Mrs. Blake told her coldly, "or exposure. Believe me, I would have absolutely no compunction about exposing this whole sordid affair. I would ruin your reputation, young lady, both here and in your home, and I would destroy my husband's teaching career. Believe me, I would do it. I will not have this affair continue."

He's property, Jackie was thinking. *That's all he is to you, Mrs. Blake, just your property. There's no love there or anything else, only a feeling of ownership, and you don't like the idea of me stealing a piece of property that belongs to you.*

At that moment, she felt more sorry for Blake than she ever had before.

Aloud, she said, "Mrs. Blake, you're right. I don't know how this ever happened, and I've been miserable ever since it started, and I think Dan—Professor Blake—I think he's been miserable and ashamed, too. It just seemed to happen, and I'm almost glad you found out. I'm almost glad it has to stop now, because it was making me nervous and ashamed and miserable. I'm glad it's over."

"Nevertheless," said Mrs. Blake, her coldness not having changed a bit, "I will not permit you to stay at this college or in this town. You must leave, and at once."

"But, Mrs. Blake—"

"At once," insisted the woman firmly.

And all of a sudden Jackie knew what she had to do. Rick, Blake, this woman, she could handle it all at once. But still she needed time. "There's only a couple weeks till exams," she said, openly pleading. "Couldn't I stay till then? I promise I won't go near your husband again, or let him come near me, but couldn't I at least finish out the semester?"

"At once," repeated the woman firmly.

"Please, Mrs. Blake."

The woman arose. "I have nothing more to say on the subject," she announced. "If you are still anywhere in this vicinity tomorrow night, I will know who to do my talking to." And with these words she stormed out of the house.

Jackie sat quietly at the kitchen table and lit a cigarette. The plan was already clear in her mind. She knew what she was going to have to do. The only question was whether

Blake would be strong enough. But he would have to be strong enough, she would have to make him strong.

As she was thinking this, Blake came into the kitchen, looking hunted and harried. "Jackie!" he cried, in a stage whisper. "Ethel was here!"

"I know damn well Ethel was here," Jackie told him bitterly. "You can't even tell when your own wife is following you. And she probably saw you come in here now, too."

"No," he said. "I came in about five minutes ago, and Laura told me Ethel was out here with you. I was hiding on the cellar stairs."

The picture of Dan Blake cowering on the cellar stairs was suddenly so ludicrous that it broke Jackie's anger and pessimism, and she got to her feet, smiling, and said, "You're good for me, Dan. Want some coffee?"

"Something stronger," he said.

She thought of what he had to do tonight, and she said, "No. You'd better stick to coffee. We have some plans to make."

"All right." He sat down at the table and quivered there, while she got the coffee. Then she sat across from him and watched him carefully. "Tell me something, Dan," she said. He looked up. "Do you love your wife?" she asked him.

"Ethel?" He shook his head. "She's just there," he said. "That's all, just there, like an albatross."

"I wanted to be sure you weren't in love with her, that's all."

"You ought to know that, Jackie," he said. "I could never love two women at the same time, and you know the only woman in the world for me is you. You don't really care anything about me, no more than Ethel does, but still—"

"That isn't true," she said suddenly. She leaned forward, putting her hand on his on the table. Her voice low, as though she were afraid of eavesdroppers, she said, "I thought you could see that, Dan. I thought you could see all that hardness was just an act."

"An act?"

"Didn't you see it, Dan?" she asked him. "I thought, at night, when we were in bed together, I thought you understood what I was doing and why I had to do it."

He shook his head. "No, Jackie, I had no idea—"

"Don't you realize, Dan? Dan, for heaven's sake, look what I've done! I was the one who made the rules here, Dan, and I've broken every one of them for you. I was the one who said a customer couldn't come to the same girl all the time, and there's only one customer who comes to the same girl all the time, and the customer is you and the girl is me.

"I was the one who said our customers would only be students from the college, and there's only one customer who isn't a student at the college, and it's you. And I was the one who said that there would never be any exception to payment, and there was only one time when someone didn't have to pay, and that was you, at the party that time after the game, the first time we went to bed together."

"Jackie, I didn't—"

"You didn't realize, Dan?" she said quickly, interrupting him. "Didn't you see that I began by liking you, and then by being sorry for you—at that same party, when that ass Ed Archer was being so loud and stupid—and finally, Dan, I came to love you." She squeezed his hand. "It's easy to love you, Dan," she murmured. "I can't understand Ethel. She must be a very frigid woman, not to be able to love you."

"But—"

"But why haven't I ever told you? Because I couldn't. Because I was afraid to, Dan."

"Afraid?" he echoed. "Afraid of what? Afraid of me? Oh, Jackie, there's no reason—"

"No," she said. "I was afraid of Rick. I'm still afraid of Rick."

She fully expected him to say, "Rick?" on a rising inflection, and he didn't disappoint her.

"Why do you think he's here all the time?" she asked him, rushing ahead, not wanting him to have too much chance to think. Once or twice as she had talked, already, she had seen momentary frowns of doubt cross his face, and she knew she had to rush on, building the web of half-truths around him, each half-truth bolstering its fellows.

"Why do you think Rick is here?" she repeated "Why do you think he gets twenty per cent of all the money that comes into this house?"

Blake's eyes widened. "I had no idea he was making any money here, Jackie," he started.

"Well, he is. He gets two dollars of every ten-dollar bill that comes into this house. And not only that." She rushed on, telling him more, telling him everything, having to build as large and as firm a base as possible, because the most difficult job of convincing him lay ahead, and the foundation had to seem secure.

"I'll tell you what else," she said. "Rick and Sandy—he's got her, too, the same way he has me—she sells marijuana for him. Right in this house. I tried to stop it. I didn't want to have anything to do with it because it's too dangerous. It could bring the police here any time, but I can't fight Rick.

He forced me to agree to it, and he forced me to sign a paper that would incriminate me in it, so I couldn't turn him in."

"Well, good God, Jackie—" started Blake.

"What could I do?" she demanded. "What could I do against him? I couldn't go to anyone for help, not the police or the college administration or anyone. How could I? How could I go to anybody and say, 'I'm a whore, and Rick Marshall is extorting some of my money from me'? How could I go to anybody for help? I couldn't."

"Jackie, if you'd told me—"

"I was afraid to, Dan. I was afraid you would get mad and you would fight him or something, and then he would go tell everyone and ruin us both. And that was why I couldn't ever show you my true feelings, either, because I was afraid of Rick.

"When I first started, when I was in the old apartment, before any of the other girls came in with me, Rick came one night and told me he was going to be my 'protector' and he wanted twenty per cent. And when I refused, he beat me up, and he forced me to say I'd help him. And there was no one to go to, no one to help me."

His face was melting, shock and sympathy and tenderness were coursing across it like tears, and she knew she had him. "My God, Jackie," he whispered. "If only you'd told me."

"He's jealous," she said. "He wants me all to himself, he doesn't want to think that any other man can be important to me or influence me. Do you remember someone named Ed Warner? A student, red-haired, I think he was in the Modes of Writing course at the beginning of the year."

Blake nodded. "I remember him. He dropped out suddenly."

"Because Rick beat him up. Because Rick threatened him and beat him up and drove him out of the school."

Blake was wide-eyed. "Could such things go on here?" he demanded. "And I used to think I knew this school. I used to think I knew what was going on around here."

"He did it because Ed was getting too interested in me," she raced on. "And because I made the mistake of letting Rick see that I enjoyed the interest. That's why he did it."

She squeezed his hand again, staring at him intensely. "Do you see now?" she asked. "Do you see why I had to hide the truth from you, why I had to play a lie for you all the time, only hoping that somehow you would be able to see it was a lie?"

"Jackie," he said breakingly, "if only you had told me—"

"I had to fight to get as much of you as I did," she said. "Rick didn't want me to let you come to the house at all, but I told him you already knew about it, since Ed Archer had brought you to the party. And then he insisted that you be treated like any other customer, that you be switched around to the different girls. I told him it was much too tricky and dangerous having you here in the first place, and it would be better if I had you stay just with me. He said, 'Don't let it go to your head, honey-girl, being in the rack with a teacher.' And I knew what he meant. He meant he'd do something to you—the way he did with Ed Warner—if it looked as though I was beginning to feel serious about you. Only maybe with you he'd just go tell your wife. That's why I've been afraid for so long."

"Jackie," he murmured. "Poor Jackie." He got to his feet and came around the table to put his arms around her and hold her close to him. "Don't worry, Jackie," he murmured. "Everything will be all right."

"But it *won't be* all right," she insisted. She pulled away from him, getting up from the table, and paced across the kitchen. "Things are even worse now," she said, "worse than they were before. I had to tell you the truth. I was so nervous after your wife came. Now Rick will find out. One way or the other, Rick will find out. And there's your wife. She threatened me and said she'd expose us both if I didn't leave school by tomorrow night. I can't bear the thought of leaving you, Dan."

"Jackie." He came across the room, arms outstretched to her. "Jackie, we don't have to stay here. We can pack up and leave, right away, tomorrow, even tonight. I can get a divorce—God knows Ethel will be happy enough to be rid of me—and we can get married. We can go a thousand miles from here."

"We never could," she replied somberly. "Oh, if only we could! But we can't, Dan, we can't. You know it as well as I do."

"Why not? We could pack and leave tonight."

"It would never work," she told him. "If we did that—and how I wish we could—but if we did it, the whole thing would blow open tomorrow. And the police would be after me, because of Rick and Sandy and the marijuana. And you'd never be able to get a job teaching again."

"Who cares about that?" he cried. "I don't care about anything but being with you."

"You'd hate me, Dan, I know you would. You're a good teacher. It's your whole life. You'd miss it, and then you'd start to blame me, and you'd end by hating me, and I wouldn't be able to bear it."

"Oh, *God*, Jackie!"

She fell into his arms, clinging to him, openly sobbing now, and inside, her brain was whirling furiously. *This is the clincher,* she was thinking. *This is the most important part. I have to do this right or I've lost everything.*

"Rick and your wife," she sobbed. "Rick and your wife. They're the only ones standing in our way. If it weren't for them, we could be happy, we could marry and I could close this house, and no one would ever have to know, and we could be happy together forever."

"Jackie, Jackie," he murmured. "We'll find some way."

"There is no way," she wept. "The two of them are there, and there's no way to get around them. Oh, if only they didn't even exist, Dan! If only they didn't exist, it would be so easy for us."

"Jackie," he murmured, clinging to her.

Abruptly she allowed herself to go rigid, and she pulled away from him and stared at him, her expression wide-eyed and frightened. "If they didn't exist," she whispered, and shook her head as though trying to get something out of her mind.

"What is it?" he asked, suddenly concerned. "Jackie, what is it?"

"How could I even think such a thing?" she asked, as though asking herself more than him. "What's happened to me, that I could even think such a thing?"

"Think what? Jackie, what's the matter? What are you thinking?"

"If they didn't exist," she whispered again, staring at him with terror on her face.

And finally he caught it, and his face paled, and he stepped back away from her. "No, Jackie! Good God, no, we couldn't!"

"Dan," she whispered. "Dan, there isn't any other way."

"There's got to be."

"There isn't any other way, Dan."

He shook his head. "That never works, Jackie. That's no answer. We'd be caught, and it would be worse than ever."

"We could do it!" she cried, exultantly, and ran to hold him again. "Listen," she whispered furiously, "I know how. I know how we could do it, Dan, and we'd never be caught. Come on, Dan, come into the bedroom. We can't let anyone else hear us. Come on!"

She led him into the bedroom, though he still kept shaking his head and mumbling that it wasn't any answer, but she knew now that she had him, that all he wanted was for her to plan the details, to tell him how the thing could be done.

And she knew how.

Sitting on the bed beside him, she outlined the plan. "I'll send Rick over there," she said. "Rick loves to beat people up, to frighten them. I'll tell him about your wife coming here tonight, and I'll tell him he'll have to go and stop her from talking. He'll love that, Dan. He's psychotic. He's always terrified me that way. Dan, listen to me. Dan, do you have a gun?"

"Jackie—"

"Do you have a gun, Dan?"

He nodded, miserably. "A hunting rifle," he said. "A thirty-thirty."

"Good. I'll tell him I'll see to it that you're out of the house at one in the morning. But you'll be there, in your bedroom, cleaning the rifle. Have all the cleaning tools spread out. But try to keep your wife from knowing you're home, because she might call for you or tell Rick you're there."

"Jackie, I couldn't do—"

"For us, Dan, for us. You've got to do it, don't you see? Now, listen, I'll have him go there at one o'clock, and you wait until you're sure it's too late to save your wife, and then you come out with the rifle and shoot Rick. Don't you see? He'll have killed her while trying to burglarize the house or something, and you shot him when he tried to get away. And no one will ever suspect because Rick has a reputation for wildness. People would believe anything about him."

"Jackie, no. It's impossible. I couldn't do it."

"There's no other way, Dan," she told him. "If we don't do it now, tonight, I'll have to leave tomorrow. We'll never see each other again. This is the only way."

She stopped talking now, let the silence grow, let him think it out for himself, and when finally he slumped forward, covering his face with his hands, she knew he was ready. She put a comforting hand on his shoulder. "You go on home now, Dan," she said, "and get everything ready. I'll have Rick get there at midnight, instead of one o'clock."

The sooner the better, she was thinking, *the sooner the better.* She didn't want him to have to wait too long, the longer he had to wait, the more time he would have to think, and the more likely he would be to remember that he was, after all, a coward.

"You know what you're going to do, don't you?" she asked him.

He nodded woodenly.

"And you'll come here tomorrow," she said, "as soon as you can. But make sure nobody follows you this time."

"I will," he said. Somehow, he managed a twisted smile. "I'm leaving," he said.

"This is the best way," she told him. "No more hiding from one another. We won't have to hide our love now."

She kissed him, passionately, and led him from the bedroom and to the back door. "Midnight," she said. "And be sure to wait until you know it's too late to save your wife."

"If only it were over," he said.

"Tomorrow, Dan."

He left and she closed the door after him, then turned to see Rita standing in the opposite doorway, staring at her. "I heard everything," the girl whispered coldly.

Oh no, thought Jackie, *not her, too, this is too much, too fast.*

"You're going to run away with him," said Rita. She took a step into the kitchen. "I heard you, I heard it all. You're going to marry him."

Jackie sighed, and plunged forward. "Don't be silly, Rita," she said. "Did you believe all that hogwash I fed Dan? I've got to get his wife out of the way, before she blows the whistle on us all, and I've got to get rid of Rick so I can be with you, and so I can have this house to myself, the way it should be."

"So you can be with me?"

"Of course." Jackie smiled, and walked across the room to take the girl's hand. *After this other thing is straightened out,* she thought, *I'll have to see about you. You know what's happening now so that's going to complicate it. But one thing at a time.* "You know better than that, don't you, Rita?" she asked. "Better than to think I'd ever leave you."

"But what you said to him—"

"I had to talk to him that way. You don't think I'd leave here and run off with a simpleton like Dan Blake, do you?"

"I was so frightened," said Rita, "when I heard you talking to him."

Jackie looked up at the clock. "It's almost ten," she said. "You'd better get ready for your customer. We can talk later."

"All right, Jackie."

"And don't you worry about anything, honey."

"I'm sorry, Jackie," the girl said contritely, her eyes warm and adoring and trustful. "I just get so silly jealous sometimes."

"Go on now. We can talk later."

Rita went away and Jackie poured herself a fresh cup of coffee. *One thing at a time,* she thought. *One thing at a time. That's the secret of success.*

She sat down at the table to wait for Rick.

8

RICK DIDN'T ARRIVE till eleven-thirty. Jackie spent the time before that in the kitchen, drinking coffee and thinking over her plans.

Around her was the house, the four girls with their customers. In the bedroom, in the locked desk drawer, was the ledger book and an envelope thick with bills—the money she had saved so far from this venture.

It could be so good, she thought. *It could be so simple and fine. But people keep horning in. People keep crowding me and complicating things.* Rick, demanding his twenty per cent and double-crossing her with Sandy to run his own private sideline in here and cheating her whenever he could. Blake, clinging to her, wanting her strength and offering nothing but his own weakness in the bargain. Rita, also clinging to her, but that, of course, she had brought on herself, and she would find the way to take care of that problem once this other thing was settled. And there was Ethel Blake, who didn't want her man for herself but refused to let anybody else have him.

People. People interfering, pushing, crowding. It could be so good and simple, running a profitable house here, putting money aside, living quietly and comfortably and happily. It could be so good and simple, and yet it had turned out to be so complicated.

Around eleven, she heard the sounds from the front of the house, the ten o'clock customers leaving and the eleven o'clock customers arriving, and the reassuring simplicity of those sounds was good for her. She would work her way through all of this mess. She was confident of that much.

But when Rick came in at eleven-thirty, she made sure she looked just as worried as possible.

He saw the expression the minute he came in, and paused, frowning. "Something wrong?"

"Everything's wrong," she told him glumly. "You'd better sit down while I tell you about it."

He came forward warily, darting a glance at the door from the kitchen to the hall, now closed, and sat down across from Jackie at the table. "Okay," he said. "What is it?"

"We had a visitor tonight," she told him

"What kind of visitor?"

"A bad kind. Blake's wife."

"His *wife?*"

"Seems she's jealous," Jackie told him. "He was spending too much time away from home. So she followed him a few times. And then she stuck around, outside, a few nights, and pretty soon she had the whole thing figured out."

"The whole thing? What do you mean, the whole thing? How much does she think she knows?"

"She knows everything," said Jackie. It wasn't true, but she wanted to give Rick as much of a sense of urgency as she possibly could. "About the business we're running here, and about you, the names of the people here and the regular customers and everything."

He sat back in the chair, and she saw him trying to keep his features composed, trying to hide just how badly this news had hit him. "That's going to be something of a problem, Jackie-girl," he said, with a pretty poor attempt at showing nonchalance.

"I know it is." She got to her feet and crossed the room to the cupboard where they kept the liquor. She took down the gin bottle, put an ice cube into a water glass, and filled it up almost to the top with gin. She brought it back to the table and set it down in front of him. "You could probably use a drink," she said. "I know I needed one or two after the woman finally decided to leave here."

"She came right in here, huh?" He picked up the glass, drank from it, and set it down again. "Came right on in."

"She sat right where you're sitting now," Jackie told him. She was glad to see that he'd taken a healthy swallow of the gin. When the police looked him over, after Blake shot him, it would be good if they could see that he had been drinking. That would help to explain why he had broken into the house in the first place, and why he had killed Blake's wife.

"So what did she have to say?" Rick asked her.

"She was mad," Jackie said.

Rick laughed and drank again. "I betcha that's an understatement, honey-girl," he said.

"You're right. But the thing was, she wasn't mad at Blake so much as she was mad at us. As though it was our fault for him coming here. It's *her* fault, if it's anybody's, but she'd never see it that way."

"That *is* the way it goes," Rick said, with exaggerated calmness, and drank again. "So she said you weren't supposed to let hubby into the house any more, is that it?"

"I wish it was as simple as that," Jackie told him.

"Now what? She wants us to close down?"

"She'll do it for us," Jackie said.

The affected nonchalance disappeared at once. "What? How do you mean that? What the hell is she going to do?"

"She's going to turn us in," Jackie said simply.

Rick slammed his palm on the table, so that the glass jumped, but the liquor level was now down far enough so none slopped over. "The hell she is!" he cried.

"I tried to talk her out of it," Jackie told him "I promised her we'd close down quietly, and I'd even leave school tomorrow, but that wasn't enough for her. She wants a scandal, she wants to punish everybody, you and me and her husband and everybody else, and she wants to punish us in a nice big public way."

"The bitch!" he cried. He drained the glass, and got to his feet to stomp around the room. "The lousy filthy bitch!" he shouted, and stopped by the workboard to pour more gin into the glass.

"It's jail," Jackie said softly. "All of us. I don't suppose I'll get more than a few months in a workhouse, and the other girls, too, but it's you and Blake I'm thinking of. I mean, I'm thinking about me, too. This is going to ruin my name, but at least I won't be in jail for very long."

He turned and glared at her. "Just what are you trying to say, honey-girl?" he asked her coldly.

"Rick, face it. You're the pimp in this crowd," she told him. "You brought Sandy into the house, and you were the one who took Rita's virginity, and you've been taking your twenty per cent every week. With me and the rest of the girls, it's just prostitution, and for all I know we might even get away with a suspended sentence. But with you it's pandering, and I think Honey is underage anyway, and that means twenty years, Rick, twenty years in jail and no way in the world of getting around it."

"Oh, that *bitch!*" he shouted. He flailed his arms, spilling gin out of the glass, then drank again and came over to slam the glass down on the table and glare—already a bit bleary-eyed—at Jackie. "I wish I'd been here," he said dangerously. "I'd have wrung the bitch's neck. I'd have torn her head off. I just wish to Christ I'd been here. Twenty years! For God's sake, I can't go to jail for twenty years! I never figured anything like this."

"Rick," she said suddenly, as though the thought had just that moment come to her. "Rick, did you mean that?"

"Did I mean what?" he demanded. He stood across from her, on the other side of the table, and the glass was in his hand again, now only half-full. "Did I mean what?"

"What you said about wringing her neck, if you'd been here? Did you mean that?"

"You're goddamned right I meant it," he shouted. "To keep from going to jail for twenty years, for Christ's sake, you're goddamn right I meant it."

"Rick," she said, sudden excitement in her voice. "Do you really think you could do it? Rick, honey, it would be wonderful if you could. I was wishing the same thing, honest to God I was, but I never thought we could really do it."

"Hold on a second," he said. He backed away and swallowed noisily, emptying the glass. "You mean kill her?" he asked, his voice suddenly high-pitched. "You mean, to really do it, to kill her?"

"Isn't that what you said, Rick? You said it yourself. I thought you really meant it. And it would solve everything, Rick, don't you see?"

"No," he said. He shook his head back and forth in an exaggerated manner. "Not on your life," he said. "What do you think I am, crazy?"

"Do you *want* to spend the next twenty years in jail?" she shrieked at him. "You'd be forty years old when you got out, Rick, think about it. Do you *want* that?"

"For God's sake, Jackie—"

"I'd do it myself," she cried. "I've been sitting here, wishing I could do it. When she was here, I looked at her, and I wished—" She stopped suddenly and whirled away, opening the drawer beneath the workboard, pulling out the large carving knife. She spun back to Rick, brandishing the knife. "I kept looking over at this drawer," she shouted. "All the time she was here, I kept looking over at this drawer, wishing I could do it, wishing I could just get up and open the drawer and take this knife out and kill her."

"For Pete's sake, Jackie, watch the knife! Watch what you're doing!" he babbled, backing away from her.

She stopped again, her body sagging, and she reached out to drop the knife heavily on the table between them. "I couldn't do it," she said, her voice low and bitter. "I wanted to, but I couldn't. And then, when you said that, I thought you could be the one. You're stronger that I am, Rick. You've always promised to take care of things for me, and I thought you could do it. I'm a coward, I admit it. I don't have the strength to do it. But I didn't know you were a coward, too."

"Jackie, *murder,* for God's sake! What do you think I am?"

"Twenty years," she said. She looked levelly at him, her eyes cold and hard. "Twenty years, for you. If you're a coward. If you can't do it."

"I'd get caught," he stammered, looking guiltily from side to side. "I'd never get away with it. Her husband would catch me, somebody would catch me."

"No!" She ran to him, holding his arm again, staring up at his face. "Rick, you could do it! Listen, Blake talked to me this afternoon, he said he wanted to come see me tonight, he said it was important. It was probably this thing about his wife. He probably wanted to warn me that she knew. I told him to get here at midnight, Rick. The house will be empty there at midnight, except for her. They don't have any children, it's just the two of them. You could go there—listen, Rick, after you did it, you could muss things up in the house a little, make it look as though it were a burglar did it. And I'll keep Blake here until you get back."

He hesitated, and she could see him considering it, weighing the alternatives, and then he shook his head definitely and said, "No. It's too risky."

She put as much scorn as she was capable of into her voice as she said, *"What* chance, Ricky? It's that, or it's twenty years."

"We could take off," he said. "We could get the hell away from here."

"And go where? Ricky, don't be a little boy. Think for once in your life. This isn't a world where you can run away, Ricky. Try to get a job somewhere, just try it. They'll want to see your Social Security card, they'll want to see your draft card, they'll want to know your work history and they'll check back on it. Unless you just want to be a ditch-digger somewhere. And the same with a house, or an apartment. The landlord always wants references. And how could you buy a car, or get a loan, or start a charge account or put money in the bank, or do anything? How could you *live*, Ricky? You aren't going to be twenty years old forever, Ricky, you've got a whole lifetime to think of. How are you going to live all your life, Ricky?"

"Don't call me Ricky!" he shouted.

She ignored him, overrode him. "How are you going to live your life, Ricky? In jail, for the next twenty years? Digging ditches and living in flophouses for the rest of your life? It's one or the other, Ricky, as long as Blake's wife is alive."

"It's too much," he said. He emptied the glass, and shook his head. "It scares me, Jackie, this is more than I ever expected. This is all too fast. Twenty years! This was just a— a kind of game, that's all. For Christ's sake, it wasn't ever anything serious, Jackie."

"It is now," she told him. "It's serious as hell, Rick. It can ruin your life."

"I don't know," he said. He reached for the gin bottle again, then shook his head and pulled his hand back from the bottle. "It scares me, Jackie," he said.

"Could you do it, Rick? You're the only one I can turn to now. Could you do it?"

"I don't know. I guess so, I *think* so. But I never expected anything like this, it shakes me up."

"But you *could* do it."

He turned and looked somberly at her, and nodded. She glanced up at the clock above the refrigerator. "It's quarter to twelve," she said. "You'll just get there in time."

"I suppose so," he said.

"Rick, are you just going to stand there? She'll go to Dean Kelland the first thing in the morning. And I won't be able to hold Blake here forever."

He shook his head again. His face was flushed now, from the gin, and it was clear that he wasn't thinking as well as usual. "I suppose so," he said again.

She picked up the knife from the table and shoved the handle into his hand. "Here. Hide it under your coat. Come *on*, Rick, there's too much at stake!"

"I suppose so," he mumbled, for the third time, and allowed her to push him out the kitchen door.

He was still holding the knife in his hand. It was a clear cold night with a three-quarter moon, and the moonlight glinted knowingly on the blade. "Hide it," she snapped, whispering now that they were outside the house. "Hide it under your coat."

"I suppose so," he mumbled again, his esses beginning to slur, and the moonlight flashed as he raised the knife and carefully slipped it, blade foremost, underneath his coat. Then he moved off the back porch and across the yard to the side street, stumbling a bit on the uneven frozen ground. She watched him until he had gone, out of sight, and then she shivered from the cold and went back into the house. She took his glass, rinsed it at the sink, dropped two ice cubes into it, and half-filled it with gin. She sat down at the kitchen table and sipped the gin.

Laura, white-faced, came into the kitchen at quarter to one. Jackie was still sitting at the kitchen table, the gin bottle now empty in front of her. She was reading and re-reading the label. Dexter's Gin, Dexter's Gin, Dexter's Gin. *Lousy gin,* she was thinking.

Laura whispered, "Jackie! There's a policeman here."

It went wrong. That was her first thought. She wondered which of them had failed, Rick or Blake, and she had the feeling she knew—it was Blake.

She got to her feet, a trifle unsteadily, and said, "What did he say?"

"He had a cigarette in his hand," Laura said. "A funny-looking cigarette, a little one. He was grinning, and he said, 'I hear this little item came from this house, is that right?' I didn't know what he was talking about, Jackie. Jackie, do you know what it's all about? He said he wanted to talk to the boss lady here."

Jackie knew what it was all about, and her profound relief at the fact that it was *not* about Blake and Rick and Blake's wife was tempered by the realization that she had been right all along, that Rick's stupid greed, his idiotic *playing* at corruption, his asinine insistence on the sale of marijuana in this house, had brought in the police.

"I know what it is," she said flatly. "I'm well aware of what it is, Laura. You go upstairs and tell the other girls not to come down for anything until I give the all-clear. And you tell Sandy that there's a policeman down here who's interested in funny cigarettes, and that if she has a brain in her head she will flush her entire stock down the toilet."

"Oh," said Laura. She was less white-faced, less frightened, now that she understood what was going on. "Sandy's had her own sideline, is that it?"

"It certainly is. Oh, and Laura."

"Yes?"

"If there's an odd smell in Sandy's room—and I'm willing to bet there will be—take that can of deodorant spray from the bathroom and soak her room good."

"Okay," said Laura. She started away, then paused to say, "Why didn't you stop her, Jackie? You know better than this."

"She's been selling it for Rick," Jackie explained tiredly. "Ever try to stop Rick from doing anything?"

"I see. Well, this should stop it."

"This just might stop everything," Jackie told her.

Laura went on upstairs, and Jackie lit a cigarette, tried to get herself under control, cursing herself for having drunk any gin tonight, and went into the living room to see the policeman.

The minute she saw him, she was no longer worried about being arrested. The only thing to worry about now was the size of the payoff.

You get rid of one leech, she thought fatalistically, *and immediately another one comes along to take his place.*

The detective was in civilian clothes. He was around forty years of age, with a barrel body tightly encased in a just-out-of-date gray suit and pointed-toe brown shoes. He had no neck, in the accepted sense of the term, just a thick rolled column that sprang up between his shoulders in support of a round heavy head. He had thinning black—hair on his high dome and a pinched-in face, small eyes set too close together beneath too-skimpy eyebrows, a small round blob of a nose, and a small thick-lipped mouth. There was too much pale skin around the central area of eyes and nose and mouth, he looked almost deformed.

The obscene mouth was smiling, showing stained teeth, and the little eyes were merry in a frightening way. "Well, well," the detective said. "So you're the one who operates this little house, is that it?"

"What do you want?" she asked him.

"Very young," he said thoughtfully, still smiling. "Surprisingly young. All college girls, is that it? I'm really surprised, you know. This looks like a going concern. I'm really surprised you managed to keep me from knowing about it this long." He nodded, smiling with fond admiration at Jackie, and said, "My name is Kober, Harry Kober. I'm a captain. I run this precinct. You know the station house, over on Prince Street?"

"I know it," she said.

"And what did you say *your* name was?" he asked.

"Jackie Hayes."

"Jackie Hayes." He savored the name, then raised one eyebrow. "Jacqueline?"

"Yes."

"Jacqueline Hayes. Very nice."

"What do you want?" she asked him again.

"You know," he said, "this really surprises me. I knew about the marijuana, but until I came here I had no idea there was more to it than that. I'm really surprised."

"All right," she said. "you're surprised." She didn't have the time or the energy to worry about this man, she wanted him to name his price, let them haggle a bit, and then he could go away and she could forget him for a while.

He had been sitting heavily on the sofa, but now he got to his feet and strolled around the living room, looking at the furniture and the walls and the rug. "Very nice place," he commented. "You just stick to the college boys, is that it?"

"Yes," she said.

"How many girls here beside yourself?"

"Four."

He nodded. "Fine. Keep any books?"

"No."

"Honor system, eh? Well, that's kids for you. What do you suppose you take in a week here, Jacqueline?"

She shrugged, "About a hundred dollars," she said.

He laughed. "Twenty dollars a girl, is that it? You charge box tops, is that the way it goes? They pay you in green stamps."

"I meant a hundred dollars each," she said.

"I see. So you really meant to say *five* hundred dollars, is that it?"

"Yes."

He nodded, smiling happily. "That's fine," he said. "That sounds about right. Ten dollars a throw, is that it?"

"Yes."

"That would be about right. And ten per cent of five hundred dollars is what, Jacqueline? You're a college girl, that should be easy for you."

"Fifty dollars," she said.

"That's right." He held out his hand. "Fifty dollars is just right," he said.

"No," she said. "We can't afford that. We have to pay the rent and everything, and we're putting ourselves through school. We can't afford that."

The smile flickered and died. "Ten dollars a week per girl?" he asked her. "That you couldn't afford. Lawyers come higher, Jacqueline, much higher. And you can't do much business in jail. Do you see what I mean?"

"It's too much," she said. She had an idea and she tried it, she had nothing to lose. She smiled at him, and stepped forward, saying, "Couldn't we work something else out? Maybe part of it in trade."

The smile of surprised admiration came back, and he said, "Why, Jacqueline! What a little businesswoman!" He glanced at the windows facing on the porch and the street and said, "Do you have an office, Jacqueline? Some place we can sit down and discuss all this?"

"Yes," she said. "Come on."

She led the way to the kitchen, and gestured to the kitchen table, but instead he went over to the closed bedroom door and pushed it open. He switched the light on and looked around, at the bed and the desk, then turned back, grinning, and said, "That your room, Jacqueline?"

"Yes. But I thought we could have some coffee and—"

"You come on in here, Jacqueline," he said.

She went, obediently, and he closed the door once she was in the room. He sat down on the edge of the bed and said, "Now, where were we? You said something about trade, I believe."

"You could have some fun," she said, forcing the smile back on her face. "Some free fun, instead of part of the money."

"I tell you what, Jacqueline," he said. "I think you've got a good idea there. But I've got a better one. I'll have the free fun, as you put it, but I'll also take my ten per cent. Now, how does that sound to you?"

"We really can't afford it, Mister Kober," she said. "Maybe twenty-five dollars and—"

"Now, don't try to haggle with me, little girl," he said. "I've told you the setup, and that's the way it is. Why don't you take that robe off?"

"Couldn't we talk about—"

"We'll see," he said. "Later, maybe." He gestured at the robe.

She didn't have any choice. She hoped he'd get it over with quickly, and then maybe he'd be more willing to talk about lowering the price. She stepped out of the robe and stood nude in front of him.

He smiled, secretively, and got to his feet. "You may find," he said, "that I have my own ideas of fun. That's the way some people are in this world, Jacqueline, they have their own ideas of fun." And his hand flicked out, a seemingly casual gesture, and slapped forehand and backhand across the tip of her breast.

She backed involuntarily into the wall, and he smiled and came after her, saying softly, "Now, you'll be quiet, won't you, Jacqueline? I won't hurt you very much, and later on maybe we can talk about money again." And the hand flicked out again, back and forth.

A cry escaped her lips, and the door shot open as Rita dashed in, face contorted with tears and rage, screaming, "Leave her alone! You leave her alone!"

Kober's look of blank astonishment was swiftly replaced by a pleased smile. "Well, what do you know," he said softly and, as Rita flung herself at him, he chopped out with the side of his rigid right hand, catching her on the side of the head, just above the ear, throwing her to the floor.

She came up clawing, sobbing with pain and fury, and hurled herself at him again, and he waited, smiling, and his hands moved with practiced pleasure.

Jackie could only lean against the wall and watch. She wanted to stop it, but she couldn't, and as long as Rita was clawing and lashing at Kober, Kober wouldn't be paying any attention to Jackie.

At last he was finished, and Rita was lying barely conscious on the floor. Kober adjusted his tie, smiled at Jackie, and said, "You didn't tell me you'd hired a whipping girl, Jacqueline. You're a smart little girl. I'll take the fifty dollars now."

She didn't argue with him. She unlocked the desk drawer, took out fifty dollars, locked the drawer again quickly before he should decide to look into it, and gave him the money.

He counted it with frustrating slowness, and then smiled again. "Fine, Jacqueline," he said. "You're a smart businesswoman. I'll come to see you again next Monday."

"I know," she said dully. All at once, she felt exhausted. She could barely think. She couldn't concentrate on this man or the threat of him or the meaning of him.

Kober glanced down at Rita and smiled at her. "A fine staff," he commented. "Admirable." And he went away.

She heard him going through the house, heard the front door open and close. And then she heard Rita sobbing.

Thank God for you, Rita, she thought all at once. *I may keep you around after all.*

As she bent to see how badly Rita was hurt, the bedroom door opened again and the other three girls crowded in, Laura looking concerned, Honey excited, and Sandy worried.

Jackie straightened up and strode across the room to Sandy. She struck the girl stingingly across the face and said, "You stupid little bitch! It was because of you! You and Rick, you two did this. He never would have come here, if it hadn't been for you."

"Rick said—" Sandy started, but Jackie cut her off, snapping, "Rick is an idiot. He's always been an idiot. Honey, you and Sandy carry Rita upstairs. See what you can do for her."

They obeyed, and soon only Laura was left. "I usually mind my own business," Laura said slowly, "but there's been a little too much happening here lately. I have the feeling it may be my business, after all. All that discussion with Dan Blake, and then the shouting you did with Rick, and now I found out that Sandy's been selling marijuana a room away from me."

"Tomorrow," Jackie told her. She suddenly felt incredibly tired. "Talk to me tomorrow."

She finally got rid of the girl and went to bed. She was asleep in seconds, and her last conscious thought was of her plan. And, for the first time, she was beginning to believe that things would not work out. Something was going to go wrong, the whole thing was going to blow up.

Maybe it already had.

9

I T HAD.

She was asleep when the pounding started at the front door. She sat up, startled, remembering everything in the first second, and her immediate thought was: *The police.*

She leaped out of bed, and the pounding started at the door again. She pulled on clothes quickly, cursing zippers and swearing at sweater arms, then dashed through the house, hoping the racket hadn't awakened the girls upstairs.

She flung the door open, and Blake stood terrified and wide-eyed on the porch. He cried, "Jackie!" and pushed his way into the house, closing the door behind him.

"What is it?" she demanded. "What went wrong?"

"I don't have much time," he gasped. "The police will be here any—"

"The police!"

"They're waiting at my place for Dean Kelland. But when they see I'm gone, they may—"

"Dan, for God's sake, what happened? Come in here!" She dragged him into the living room, switching on lights, and grabbed his wrist to look at his watch. It was quarter after two. She'd been asleep less than half an hour—Kober had been gone no more than forty-five minutes.

"Now," she said. "What happened?"

"I'm sorry, Jackie," he stammered again. "When I saw them—when I heard Ethel—"

"From the beginning," Jackie ordered. She was fighting down the demand for urgency. "You left here, you went home. Did you manage to be home without your wife knowing it?"

He nodded miserably. "I went home, and then I told her I was going down to the bar for a while. You know, where I drink with Ed Archer sometimes. I thought she'd follow me, so I went there really, and then I went out the back way and sneaked home. She was in the living room, so I could get into the house through the kitchen door and go upstairs. I did everything just the way you suggested, Jackie, everything. I spread out the ramrod and the linseed oil and everything on the bed, got my rifle out, and waited."

"Then he came," she said. "And killed your wife. And then what?"

"No," he said. He covered his face with his hands. "That's just it. I couldn't let it happen. When it came right down to it, I couldn't let it happen."

She glared at him, her eyes hard and cold. "What did you do, Dan? Tell me. What did you do?"

"She—she cried out. I heard him come in, and then she cried out, and—" He raised his face suddenly, turning to stare at Jackie, his eyes pleading for understanding. "She's my wife, Jackie. She's my *wife.*"

"You stopped him," she said. It wasn't a question, she already knew the answer.

"I had to. I couldn't help it. I saw him there—he was holding the knife and struggling with Ethel, and—I just couldn't help it, Jackie."

"You shot him," she said, "before he killed your wife."

"No." He shook his head, and his eyes left Jackie's face, never stopped their pleading for her understanding and forgiveness. "I didn't shoot him, Jackie. I couldn't."

She shook her head. "You couldn't," she said. "Don't tell me what you did instead, Dan. Let me guess. You called the police."

"Ethel called," he said. "I came in with the rifle—I meant to shoot him, Jackie, I swear to God I did!—but I came in, and he was half-drunk, weaving around, struggling with Ethel, the two of them fighting for the knife, and I just shouted at him, and he backed away from Ethel, dropping the knife, and then she called the police."

"Then what?" Jackie asked woodenly.

"We waited for the police. And he said, 'She was supposed to keep you away.' He kept saying that."

Jackie closed her eyes. "Your wife was there? She heard him?"

"She asked him who he meant, who was supposed to keep me away."

"And he told her." Jackie looked back at Blake again. "That's right, isn't it? He told her it was me. And then she started in on you, and Rick kept on talking, and pretty soon your wife knew everything. And you did your own talking, I suppose, telling Rick that I had sent you to kill him—"

"No, Jackie, no. I didn't tell him a thing. Ethel found out everything. He just kept talking about it—he thought she already knew about the house here, that's what you'd told him, that she already knew—so he just kept talking about it until she did know. He was half-drunk, and he just kept talking about it. I couldn't stop him."

"You couldn't stop him." She got to her feet. "You couldn't do anything, could you, Dan? You couldn't wait for Rick to be finished, and you couldn't shoot him, and you couldn't stop your wife from calling the police, and you couldn't stop Rick from talking. You couldn't do anything, could you?"

"Jackie, I didn't know how it was going to be," he pleaded. "Sitting up there in the room, waiting—it kept gnawing at me and gnawing at me." He stood up beside her, clutching at her hands. "Jackie, come on, we can still go away from here. The two of us, we can still get out of here."

"No," she said shortly. "I told you last night what it would be like. We'll just have to think of something. Her mind was churning furiously, as she assessed the extent of the damage, saw the wreckage of her plans strewn around her. "We can still work something out," she said abstractedly. "You wait here, Dan, I'll be right back. For God's sake don't go anywhere."

"I'll wait here," he promised.

She left him and moved rapidly through the house to the kitchen and thence to her own room. It was all over and she knew it. Rick would have figured out the double cross by now, and if she knew Rick he would be doing everything in his power to get even with her.

And it wouldn't be all that difficult. All he had to do was open his mouth and start talking to the police. To the police. He could tell them about the house here, that Jackie was the madam. And he could—he undoubtedly would, to get himself off the hook as much as possible—tell them about the marijuana, and say that that was Jackie's idea, too. And he could tell them about tonight—all he had to do was tell them the truth about tonight.

He would tell them that Jackie had lied to him, that Jackie had said that Ethel Blake knew everything and was going to turn them in. And then the police would check with Ethel Blake, and they would find out that she hadn't known anything about the whorehouse until after Rick had attacked her, and then they would begin to wonder why Blake had been cleaning his rifle at midnight of a weekday, and they would very soon figure out that one person they really ought to see would be Jackie Hayes.

And now Dean Kelland was in on it, too. The police were waiting at Blake's place for him—they'd already called him. He and Ethel Blake and Rick and the police, everybody talking and listening, and the police probably knew all about it by now, that was why they'd called Dean Kelland.

They'd be coming here. They'd be coming here any minute. They'd know that this was where Blake would be coming, and they would race here just as fast as they could, the police and Dean Kelland.

And Jackie Hayes was determined to be gone before they arrived.

Once in the bedroom, she unlocked the desk drawer and removed the ledger book and the envelope full of money. Holding the envelope, she thought of the fifty dollars she had paid to Kober. What a waste that had turned out to be, after all. She had bought useless protection. Even if he wanted to, Kober would no longer be in any position to avoid arresting her.

She stuck the ledger book and the envelope into her overnight bag, zipped the bag shut, and moved quickly and stealthily across the kitchen and out the back door. The MG was parked in the driveway beside the house—there was no garage—and she hurried to this, put the overnight bag down behind the seat, and went back around and into the kitchen again.

There was only one thing left to do. Convince Blake to wait here and stall them for her. What would she tell him?

That she was going to go after a lawyer. She would tell him that she was going to go talk to a lawyer, and then she would come back, and that she would even bring the lawyer back with her if she could. Blake would want to come with her, but she could tell him that it would be too dangerous for anyone to see the two of them together. So he would wait here, and soon the police would come, and Blake would assure them that Jackie was coming back soon, Jackie had only gone away for a little while to see a lawyer. That would give her enough of a head-start. She had no idea yet where she was going, but she would have the head-start, and that would be all she would need.

She went into the house, through the kitchen and along the hall, and stopped at the threshold of the living room, staring at Captain Harry Kober.

Blake was in the room, too. Blake and Kober. Blake and Kober and three other policemen—these three in uniform—and Dean Kelland. They were all looking at her, and when she saw them she must have stepped involuntarily back, because Kober said, "Don't go away, young lady. We want to do some talking with you."

I'm supposed to make believe I don't know him, she thought. Kober's face was hard and cold, without the evil merriment of last night, and she knew the man was worried—terrified that she would say the wrong thing.

Blake was still sitting where she had left him, on the sofa, looking more terrified and miserable and inadequate than ever. Dean Kelland—tall, spare, white-haired and patrician-looking—stood as rigid as a retired army colonel. The three uniformed policemen eyed the other occupants of the room with blank-faced disinterest.

Dean Kelland spoke, his voice booming with the sound of the trained orator. "Yes," he boomed, "do come in here, Miss Hayes. You have some explaining to do." His cold, old eyes fell on Blake. "As does Professor Blake," he said.

Blake winced at the sound of his voice, but he didn't look up.

Jackie stepped forward into the room. This was too much. It was happening too fast, it was unfair, this was too much. "And so does Harry Kober have some explaining to do," she snapped.

"I have no idea what that means, young lady," Kober said quickly. "But if you think you'd like to be abusive, I suggest you just let that wait for a while. There are a number of other matters first. Such as the fact that you are quite apparently the proprietor of a brothel."

"In all my years as an educator," boomed Kelland stentorianly, "I have never seen anything like this. I could never have *imagined* such a thing."

"There's also this business about narcotics being sold here," Kober went on, "and the fact that you conspired to commit two murders."

"And the fact," Jackie snapped, too enraged to care, knowing only that she wanted to spread the guilt as far as possible, "that you came here no more than an hour ago and extorted fifty dollars from me for keeping quiet about this brothel of mine and the selling of narcotics here, and then started to beat me up, just for fun, because that's the way you get your fun."

"I don't know where you think an idiotic story like that is going to get you," said Kober, unruffled. "I've never been in this house before in my life. If I had been aware of your activities in my precinct, I would certainly have stepped in and closed you long ago."

"Personalities of her type," boomed Kelland, "have a habit of trying to make the rest of the world appear as black as themselves."

"It's true," Jackie said. "And I can prove it."

"Can you?" asked Kober, smiling as though indulging a willful child. "With bruises, perhaps? I don't seem to see any bruises on you, from this beating you claim I gave you. Or perhaps I signed a receipt for the money I extorted from you."

"This is absurd," boomed Kelland. "She has simply succeeded in diverting us away from the questions at hand."

"I don't have the bruises," Jackie snapped, "but someone else has. You started to beat me, and another girl stopped you, and then you beat her instead."

"I see," said Kober, smiling and nodding. "And this girl—unfortunately—isn't available right now to show us her bruises. Is that the story?"

"No, it isn't," Jackie told him. "She's here all right." She turned to the stairs and shouted, "Rita!"

"Well, really," said Kober. "Do you actually have a girl upstairs who fell down or some such thing, and you're going to try to blame me for the result?"

"Rita, come down here!"

"The time has come to talk," boomed Kelland. "We've had enough of this nonsense."

He might have kept talking, but at that moment Rita reached the landing, and could look down at the people in the living room. The shriek she gave at seeing Kober, the sudden whitening of her face, the involuntary backward step she made, were all much more telling proof of the truth of what Jackie had said than any bruises would have been, though the bruises were there, too, on her face, the black eye and the cut cheek.

Kelland stepped forward suddenly, looking from Kober's startled face to Rita's terrified appearance, and he said, "What is this? Is it true? What is this?"

"Dean Kelland!" cried Rita. She moved all at once, hurrying down the stairs, and running forward to cling to his arm. "I'm glad!" she cried. "I'm glad you're here. I'm glad it's over! That filthy man, and Jackie having to pay Rick and everybody, and that man Blake around all the time—and I could never sleep, I was always afraid. I knew somebody would find out some day, and I'm glad it's over. I'm glad it's finally over!"

Blake roused himself at last, coming up from the sofa with a face red with rage, staring at Kober. "You scum!" he cried. *"I* was trying to help her, at least. Whatever I've done wrong, I was trying to help her. But *you*—" And he leaped at Kober.

Two of the uniformed policemen grabbed Blake and held him back, and when Kober started suddenly for the door, the other policeman intercepted him, and they struggled noisily in the doorway. Rita was still sobbing out her story to Dean Kelland, and for the moment no one was watching Jackie.

The moment was all she needed. One backward step and she was out of the living room and into the hall. Three more steps and she was through the doorway to the kitchen. Six running steps took her across the kitchen, and then she was out and dashing over the back porch and around the yard to the side of the house and down to the MG.

She jumped behind the wheel, and as she started the engine she felt movement beside her, and turned her head to see Rita sitting in the bucket seat at her right. "I got away!" Rita cried, "they were all fighting in there, and Dean Kelland was shouting at them all to stop, and I got away."

Jackie had no time for her now. She thought quickly that she would have time to get rid of the stupid girl later, and then her foot jammed down on the accelerator and the MG leaped out to the street.

The uniformed policemen were running across the front porch as she careened out of the driveway, and Blake was running behind them, shouting Jackie's name and waving frantically, his arms pinwheeling around his head.

Jackie spun the wheel hard, and the MG climbed the opposite curb, then bounced down to the pavement. She got it back under control and headed down the night-deserted street for the highway.

In the rear-view mirror, she could see them. They milled around in front of the house for a minute, and then they ran to their police car and started after her. But she was four blocks away before their car started into motion.

She knew she could keep ahead of them, and that she would be able to lose them.

She went two more blocks, running without headlights, then made a corner on two wheels, and Rita screamed, clinging to the seat and the dashboard as the car lifted at an angle and the pavement was a gray blur rushing by just below her face.

By the time she got to the highway, their headlights were only a distant blur behind her, and she took the secondary road that led away north to another main highway. She flicked on her lights—no one followed her.

She was away clear.

Yes, she thought, she was away clear. And just what was she away clear with? A car, for one thing. A car with known license plates, that she would have to get rid of before too very long, because there would be an alarm out for her, not just in Ohio but in all the states around Ohio. So she had a car, but the car was very soon going to be useless.

And she had Rita. She had Rita, and she was going to have to get rid of Rita, too, because Rita was only going to slow her down and insure that she got caught. And there wouldn't be any gentle way to get rid of Rita—she was too busy worrying about other things to be gentle to Rita—and that meant that Rita would be mad at her, and Rita would be able to tell the police what direction Jackie was going in.

And she had not quite six hundred dollars, in an envelope in the overnight bag behind the seat.

That was all. That was all she had to show for all the work and all the strain and all the trouble she had gone to. Six hundred dollars, a car that could betray her and a girl who *would* betray her.

She didn't have the Maple Street house, and the girls working for her, she didn't have the money and the ease, she didn't have college, she didn't have any of the things she had wanted.

And why not? Because of men. Because of men like Rick, and Blake, and Kober. Because of men.

The more she thought, the angrier she became, and the angrier she became the harder she drove. She remembered that night, long ago, when Rick had first suggested this whole thing to her, when she had been mad at the thought of having to leave school, and she had driven out her anger the way she liked to do, and Rick had clung to the seat and his face had been pasty with the fear he was too proud to voice.

She glanced over at Rita, and saw that Rita, too, was terrified, just as Rick had been, and she was glad of it. She pressed the accelerator farther, and they roared along the secondary road toward the main highway, screaming through the curves and whistling down the corkscrew grades.

They had taken it all away from her. Men had taken it all, and now they were hunting her, and she was enraged at men, and glad to be punishing Rita, and furiously exhilarated by the rush and motion of the car, and they tore around a curve far too fast, the same thing that had happened with Rick that time, the rear wheels catching in the gravel at the shoulder of the road and spinning furiously.

And dropping from gravel to sand.

And the car seemed, slowly, so slowly, to rise into the air, curling and turning lazily over, and Jackie could look out and away, far, far away beyond the hood, down the long slope covered with trees that fell away to the left of the road. The car lifted up and out and over so slowly that it seemed to take all eternity.

And Rita screamed for the last time.

And when the car stopped, it burst into flame, and Jackie knew that no one would ever spend the six hundred dollars.

About the Author

Edwin West is the pen name of a popular writer who has written many short stories and who has two hardcover novels to his credit, both published by Random House. He has lived most of his life in New York City and during the warmer months spends part of his time away from his typewriter playing bit parts in summer stock with his wife, who is an accomplished actress.

To see our other great titles,
visit us at:

BLACKBIRD BOOKS
www.bbirdbooks.com